Metaphorosis

December 2023

Beautifully made speculative fiction

Also from Metaphorosis

Metaphorosis Magazine

Metaphorosis: Best of 20xx
Metaphorosis 20xx: The Complete Stories
annual issues, from 2016
Monthly issues

Plant Based Press

Best Vegan Science Fiction & Fantasy
annual issues, 2016-2020

from B. Morris Allen:
Chambers of the Heart: speculative stories
Susurrus
Allenthology: Volume I
Tocsin: and other stories
Start with Stones: collected stories
Metaphorosis: a collection of stories

Verdage

Reading 5X5 x3: Changes
Reading 5X5 x2: Duets
Score: an SFF symphony
Reading 5X5: Readers' Edition
Reading 5X5: Writers' Edition

Vestige

The Nocturnals, by Mariah Montoya

Joyful Heave

Museum Piece: an unusual collection

Metaphorosis

December 2023

edited by
B. Morris Allen

ISSN: 2573-136X (online)
ISBN: 978-1-64076-271-8 (e-book)
ISBN: 978-1-64076-272-5 (paperback)

Metaphorosis
a magazine of speculative fiction
from
Metaphorosis Publishing

Neskowin

December 2023

Visions for the Independent City of New York

Cidney Mayes

Addie Bell was six years old when she first held colored drawing pencils between her uncoordinated fingers and made marks on a crumbling map of the old, flooded tunnels beneath the city. It was a typical pastime for a child of her age, but looked different depending on what district of the Independent City of New York the child found themself living in. If Addie had resided in the Cloud District, she would have colored with a stylus on a tablet, swiping in a palette of pixels to drop red into the waiting outline of an apple on her device. Her street would have been clean, her clothes pristine, and the top of her house would have reached like a golden chapel into the sky. If she had lived in the Mids, Addie would have sat in a clump of other children her age, sharing supplies, and fighting over who would get to use their orange pencil to color in the sweet fruit on their alphabet worksheet. Her father would have had a blue-collar job and kept things in the Cloud District running smoothly. He would have been compensated well for his services. Instead, Addie Bell was one of the few children in the Deep, the level of the city that sat closest to the polluted water, to own such a nicety as colored pencils and thought herself very lucky to have such a treasure.

Addie's father, Charlie, was a weathered man with gnarled, arthritic hands who walked the dank streets collecting all manner of items. An accident on an oil rig had robbed him of good posture, unable to perform the necessary heavy lifting out at sea, so he walked the streets and shores looking for things to sell, objects dropped by those who lived above or washed up on the street banks with the tide. Items that would fetch a good price with the junkman were quickly sold, but occasionally he would bring home a gift to his daughter. It was just the two of them who lived in a city-appointed, wooden shack that could not keep out the damp. When he saw the pencils on a grimy street corner, fallen through a grate in the scaffolding above that held the rest of the city aloft, he pocketed them.

His daughter's rise to fame, and subsequent tragic fall, was not something he anticipated when he handed her the mildewed, tattered box of half-used drawing pencils.

Addie was fascinated with her new colors. Boxes, scraps of paper, and even the walls of their shack became her canvas, filled with faintly drawn shapes and lines. She knew that it would be very hard for her father to find more of the magic pencils, so she used them lightly, delicately, leaving whispers of luminous color one might miss unless they looked carefully.

The day after her father had given her the pencils, Addie went with her neighbor, Mrs. Martinez, while her father went off to pick through flotsam. Together, Addie and Mrs. Martinez walked for half an hour up the winding, unsteady steps to the lower Mids to take their usual spot. While Mrs.

Martinez, a short woman with ink-black hair and a kind face, thrust her wooden cup into the path of passersby, pleading for alms, Addie entertained herself by drawing on the cracked concrete, relishing the soft scratch of her pencil against the pebbly surface. Mrs. Martinez's benefactors were quick to give Addie a bit of their change, too, amused and maybe a little wistful that she knew nothing yet of life's hardships and cruelty. Addie accepted the coins shyly, placing them with a muted *clink* into her dress pocket.

She dutifully gave the coins to her father that night. She didn't need them. She had her magic pencils. Besides, her father used the money to buy them something good to eat. Slices of not-too moldy bread and pale cheese, which they toasted over their stove. Addie drew a picture of herself and her father, eating their cheesy toasts together, which he accepted with wet eyes and pinned to the wall of their shack.

Everything changed the day a city official, clothed in white and carrying a tablet that glowed blue, meandered down the street.

He stopped occasionally, making notes on his screen, and commiserating with his assistant about the poor conditions of the Lower Mids. Addie watched out of the corner of her eye and noted that the hem of his pristine robe was smeared with dirt. He mumbled to his assistant, something about 'real change this term'. He stopped in front of Addie's spot and cocked his head, staring at her with the curiosity of a cat watching a fish floundering in the shallows.

Addie kept her eyes fixed on her work. She drew faces of people on the street with surety, tiny birds who rummaged through the trash bin with realistic detail, and the market streets of the Mids with captivating perspective. Her drawings had a strange, bright quality due to her odd color choices. Addie felt the hair on the back of her neck prickle as the man watched her. Finally, he cleared his throat, and asked, "Child, what is your name?"

"Addie Bell," she replied, not looking up from her work. People around them grew quiet. Mrs. Martinez clutched her wooden cup and took a few steps closer to her charge.

The city official, more astute than his peers who had never left their borough in the skies, sensed the uneasiness at his presence. The citizens were wary of his pointed interaction. "Well, Addie Bell, might I commission you to draw something for me?" He held a silver coin between two fingers. It caught the light, and the small crowd grew larger.

Addie looked up from her work then, sensing the shift in the air. Her face pinched in confusion. She had seen men in pristine, pale clothing walking in the streets every once in a great while, but never had any of them spoken to her. Nor had she ever seen a silver coin before. "I only trade for 3 coppers," she said nervously.

The crowd tittered as the city official flashed a toothy smile. Addie's cheeks flushed; her stomach flipped. She felt suddenly self-conscious. Everyone was looking at her.

"I see. This is worth two hundred coppers. If you draw what I ask for, you are welcome to keep the extra." He kept the smile plastered on his face as his assistant withdrew a smaller tablet and held it in front of her, capturing the interaction on video.

Addie looked to Mrs. Martinez for confirmation of this sum, who gave her a tight nod. "Okay. What would you like me to draw?"

"Have you ever seen the city from a distance away, where all the buildings can be seen together, reaching into the sky?"

Addie shook her head as her eyes pricked with tears. She didn't understand what the man wanted, and everyone was still staring. All she knew how to draw was what she saw, and she had no idea how to draw what he wanted.

"Let me show you." The city official swiped his fingers around his tablet and flipped it around for her to see the photo of the city's skyline.

Addie stared at the picture for thirty seconds, taking in the shapes and details of the buildings that stacked on top of one another, clawing for purchase, trying to escape the rising sea beneath them. "Okay," she said, once she had memorized all she needed to. She spread a clean sheet of paper on the concrete and began to draw, now oblivious to the swell of people around her. Addie grabbed colored pencils, seemingly at random, as the buzz from the crowd fell into the background. She used her whole arm to draw wide swaths of color, painting the sky in a frenzied rainbow, then placed the buildings against it, exactly as she had seen in the photo.

When she was done, she stood and placed her hands on her hips, scrutinizing her work. Satisfied, she handed the drawing to the city official as his assistant took a photo of the exchange. Everyone clapped politely. The city official handed the silver coin to Addie, who thought it felt very heavy, and left with his drawing. The crowd dispersed, and Addie and Mrs. Martinez bought a hearty dinner to bring home, as well as a sealed box of brand-new colored pencils which Addie clutched tightly to her chest.

The video, artfully edited by the official's press team, went viral the next day. The drawing was posted to the city official's website with the tagline *a vision of what the Independent City of New York could be*. Cloud District citizens, as well as Upper Mids, loved it. The comments poured into all social channels, hashtags trended, and approval ratings went up, up, up.

Addie was unaware that anything had changed. The next day, she and Mrs. Martinez returned to their street corner and went about their business as usual. They did not know that the city official was very astute and knew just how to keep the buzz going. He made some calls and secured for Addie Bell a scholarship to a prestigious STEAM Academy where science, technology, engineering, art, and mathematics students studied to become the next generation of city leaders.

More men wearing cloud-white uniforms appeared that afternoon, stepping out of a black car. Addie felt her stomach twist into knots as they approached. Mrs. Martinez stepped in front of her, blocking her from their view. It took some convincing for Mrs. Martinez to move aside and let them talk to the young girl. They asked where her father was, and when she told him, one of the men scrunched up his nose like he'd gotten too close to the Deep's standing water. With Addie leading them, they descended rickety stairs to the banks of the Deep.

Her father stood, arms crossed and shabby clothes hanging from his thin frame, as the official's men showed him a piece of paper with a shiny seal. They spoke of moving, of government allowances, of giving Addie *opportunity*.

Addie's father stood as still as stone, distrustful. He believed it was all a sham until they showed him the viral video, and asked Addie herself. "Wouldn't you like to go to school? To take some art classes?"

Addie's eyes grew wide. She nodded, unable to speak. Mrs. Martinez often spoke of school. It sounded like a wonderful place.

Seeing Addie's face, her father finally set down his collection bucket, grabbed his daughter's hand, and followed the men. Mrs. Martinez and their neighbors watched them go, with smiles that did not quite reach their eyes.

Another video aired on the city broadcast. It was a compilation of quick cuts set against an uplifting song, showing Addie accepting her scholarship, moving into a house on the outskirts of the Cloud District with her father, and walking past the gates of the STEAM Academy. Her life, compressed into a forty-second press piece, could not convey the unbridled joy she felt as she stepped into her first art class, how her heart fluttered against her ribs, how her fingers itched to draw.

In the Academy, students sat in a ring, their heads bowed like acolytes before their easels. Each flicked their eyes towards the center of their circle, observing a bowl of fresh fruit set before them. A white-robed instructor sat Addie before an easel and told her to draw. The next two hours flew by in a blur of color and shape. Addie had never known such peace, to sit and draw undisturbed, listening to gentle music.

At the end of the class, the work was critiqued. Addie listened as students commented on one another's shading techniques, use of color, or perspective. Addie's drawing was last. It left the class speechless. She did not simply draw the fruit and the table on which it sat like everyone else. She drew her view of the whole room, including the instructor as he paced between easels, the students at worship before their own art, the sweeping pillars that held the ceiling aloft, in her signature display of churning color.

Addie twisted her hands, nervous at their silence. Tears stung the corners of her eyes as her fear and shame grew. Her art did not look like everyone else's.

"It is extraordinary," the instructor finally declared, and students began hounding Addie with questions. They clapped her on the back, praised her composition, and marveled at her color palette. Addie smiled so wide that her cheeks began to hurt and felt as if her chest could burst from happiness.

After that, people began to call Addie Bell *singularly talented, visionary*, and *genius*. A month went by, then two, and Addie settled into her new life. She and her father took to spending their weekends in the park, taking picnics of fresh fruit and bread. Addie like to draw her father sitting in the grass, running his hands through it, marveling at its softness, head tipped to welcome the sun on his skin. In the Deep he'd always been hunched, plagued with coughing spasms. A visit to the doctor had finally cleared the ailment in his chest, and he now breathed much more easily. While Addie went to school, he got a job in the Mids sorting scrap metal in a factory. It wasn't glamorous work, but he made a decent wage and was home in the early evening to share supper with his daughter and listen to her talk excitedly about her day.

As she grew up, Addie became the most celebrated artist in her school. Requests for her artwork poured into the Academy from Cloud District citizens, for everyone with taste wanted a Bell original for their homes. Her instructors encouraged her to examine the world around her, noting the line, shape, and shadow of her environment. Addie drew and painted, observing her subjects closely. And the more she saw, the angrier she became.

It started with small things, trivial points of friction with her classmates. The other students who grew up in the sun and sky knew nothing of the damp that swallowed those who lived below them in the Deep. They teased her for being an outsider, then grew jealous when she stole all the attention of her art teachers. She did find friends, and enjoyed spending time with them, but they could never understand where she had come from. When she tried to tell them what it was like growing up in the Deep, she was met with uncomfortable silence. Such things were not talked about. The news did not even mention any happening south of the Mids. "Well, you live here now," they would say, and the conversation quickly moved on to shopping and crushes.

Her father did not like to linger on the past, either. Addie could not bear the pain in his eyes when she tried to bring it up. So, the picture in her mind of the Deep grew faded and fuzzy, time softening the harshness of her memory. But she always thought fondly of Mrs. Martinez and wondered how she was doing. It did not seem right to bury the past so easily, so she kept the dulled shards of her memories, the jabs from her classmates, their lack of understanding, pressed tight against her ribs where they pricked her heart when she lay in bed, trying to find sleep.

On the day of her sixteenth birthday, the dulled shards of her pain were sharpened to razor points when she saw the news. The broadcast played on the screen in her room as she dressed for school. There was no way to change the channel. The broadcasts came at scheduled intervals, morning and night, regardless of if they were wanted or not. The reports reminded them all how lucky they were, and the dangers of what happened when one strayed too far from the confines of the Cloud District. This morning, the broadcast was a tale of the latter. A report on a crackdown of panhandling in the lower Mids, an effort for city-wide improvement.

Addie watched in disbelief, hairbrush halfway through her tresses, as Mrs. Martinez flashed across the screen. She, and a few other faces she recognized, were moved off their street corner by Cloud guards. The old woman's hair was streaked with silver, the lines of her face deep with dismay, her back hunched, but there was no mistaking her. Time had not been as kind to her as it had to Addie.

With trembling hands, Addie tied her hair into its neat twist. She hugged her father goodbye, slung her bag over her shoulder, and marched to school. Her thoughts were in tangles. At the beautiful gates where she had nearly wept with joy upon first seeing them, she felt her cheeks flush and acid creep up her throat. Her feet were cemented to the sidewalk. The sight of Mrs. Martinez's face had rattled something deep within her, and Addie could not make herself go inside. Instead, she turned on her heel and began the very long walk out of the Clouds.

Addie strode past the towering, gilded homes to the first flight of stairs made of cement and iron. Down she went, minutes turning to hours, descending to the Mids. The smell of standing water filtered up from the Deep even here. It stung her nose and sharpened those memories that had gone as soft and blurry as blended pastels. Her shoes were dirty and stained by the time she reached the corner where she'd spent her days drawing on the rough concrete. Mrs. Martinez was nowhere to be found. There were very few people around and the street was oddly quiet, given that it was midday. Addie hadn't really expected her to be here. She took a long breath through her nose, adjusted her school bag, and took the rickety stairs back down to the Deep, ignoring the strange looks from passersby.

The shack was smaller than she remembered. Addie rapped on the rough wooden door with her knuckles, and a faint voice called through it. "Who's there?"

Addie spoke past the lump in her throat. "It's Addie, Mrs. Martinez. Addie Bell."

The door opened a crack. Only Mrs. Martinez's wide eyes were visible. "Oh, mija, it's really you. Come in, quick."

Addie stepped inside the shack and took the offered seat on a three-legged stool. Mrs. Martinez sat on her bed with a groan. "Mija, what are you doing here? Don't you have school? A smart girl like you shouldn't be missing your classes."

"I came to see how you were doing." Addie decided not to tell her that the reason for her visit was because she had seen her on the broadcast, and that she wanted to relieve herself of the invisible guilt that she carried with her. She had thought that seeing Mrs. Martinez would make her feel better. It only made her chest ache.

Mrs. Martinez's eyes darted to the door. "That's very sweet, but I think you should go back home." She inhaled a wet, raspy breath and coughed, her body shaking under the attack.

Addie stood, alarmed. She sounded worse than her father ever had. "You should see a doctor," she said, once the coughing had subsided.

"No doctor will see me," Mrs. Martinez croaked.

"Why not?"

"I don't have insurance."

Addie narrowed her eyes. "What's insurance? You're sick. Papa saw a doctor and ..." Addie stopped at the sad look that passed across her former caretaker's face. Her cheeks burned, mortified. Of course, her father had only seen a doctor when they moved into their Cloud house. "I'm sorry," she said softly.

"It's okay. I'm glad you came to see me. I've missed you, but you really should be in school."

Addie stood and gathered her bag. "You're right. I'm happy I got to see you. Bye, Mrs. Martinez." She gave the old woman a careful hug and left. Instead of heading towards the shaky stairway, she walked along the damp, grimy streets of the Deep, stopping when she reached the sickly lapping of the water's edge. Had it always been this far up the street?

She stood, gazing out past the gloom of the rusty beams that held the city aloft. The water sloshed in and out, reeking of sewage and decay. A dead seagull, wings akimbo, floated nearby.

Whispers of dissent had been bubbling up from the Deep for some time. She had overheard her classmates, the children of government officials, share stories in hushed voices. They spoke of strikes, protests, retaliation. The ember of anger that had ignited in her chest this morning turned into a roaring flame. The sea was eroding homes, eating away at their crumbling foundations, yet the Mids did not welcome the people who lived in the Deep into their level of the city. Addie could not imagine the Clouds ever doing anything to help.

She looked at her shoes, stained from her trek. Shame made her eyes prick with tears. She'd been so blind; dazzled by the sparkling life she'd been given. Why had she been chosen, out of all the people here, to move up to the Clouds? Addie felt, suddenly, that she did not deserve it.

That night at home as she lay in bed, unable to sleep, she searched for her own name on her tablet. She found a video that had aired after her first art class. A reporter had taken a short clip of Addie with her still-life drawing, the one she'd been so proud of on her first day. When asked about the nature of her composition, she replied that she'd drawn what she saw. She scrolled and found the video from the city official, the one with the tagline, *a vision of what New York could be.*

Addie pushed herself out of bed and hastily cleared her worktable. She grabbed her colored pencils and began to draw a copy of her own artwork. She drew it nearly identical to the original, with swirling colors and the city skyline. Only this time, she added a slashing line of blue: the ocean rising to swallow the city, bodies floating in the water. She scrawled *a vision of what New York WILL be* across it in jarring red.

By the time she was done, the sun was just beginning to rise. Addie readied herself for school, ignoring the broadcast that played yet another cautionary tale. She placed her newest piece into her portfolio, tucking it safely between other drawings. Addie hugged her father a little tighter than usual as she said goodbye.

While everyone else was in their classes, Addie stole away to the workroom. She made dozens of copies of her newest piece, printing bundles of flyers which she shoved into her bag. Lastly, she made a large banner, wider than her arms and half as tall as she was. Perspiration beaded on her brow as the laser printer did its work, rolling out her print one inch at a time. It finished just as morning classes were dismissed. Her heart pounded in her ears as she rolled up the giant banner and marched back out the school gates.

She walked, head held high, straight to the heart of the Cloud District. At every corner, she tossed a few flyers from her bag, marring the pristine streets. She moved quickly, not stopping to hear the shocked murmurs at her behavior, or the fearful whispers of rebellion. A little drone began to follow her once she was three blocks away from her destination. She broke into a run, anxiety making her swift.

On the steps of the capital, Addie dropped her school bag and rolled out her banner. The drone had caught up with her and was now beeping shrill commands. Heavy footsteps sounded on the marble steps, but Addie did not look up from her work. She pushed the paper until it unfurled across the stairs. She stood, hands on her hips, studying her work. She could not hear the shouts above the sound of her own pounding heart, but she felt hands grab her roughly at the elbows. She was steered into a car that hovered off the street by Cloud guards, their faces obscured by helmets.

Addie did not feel scared until they escorted her to a windowless, white room that smelled of antiseptic. Her stomach clenched in fear as they pinched her arm with a needle that put her to sleep, and set about dissecting what had given this girl from the Deep the audacity and to paint the world in such colors.

Addie Bell's fall from grace was a brief news headline on the evening broadcast. Too many people had seen the flyers for the incident to not be addressed. It made for a wonderful cautionary tale. Clouds sneered at their screens and removed their Bell originals from their walls in shame, for the little girl from the Deep had no real talent at all. It was, in fact, a horrible anomaly of her vision that distorted her way of viewing the world. For Addie Bell was colorblind and did not perceive the world as those with all their proper eye cones did. She had been picking colors blindly, scribbling nonsense onto her canvases. There was no real *vision* there at all. And her vulgar art did not paint the whole picture, the effort the city was making to stem the rising seas, to help clean up the streets of the lower districts. The Clouds washed their hands of her and went about their lives.

Addie was questioned. The government wanted to know whom she was working with, who had given her orders to destroy her own art. Her answers were simple, and honest. After a few hours of questioning, when they had given up trying to extract names of other dissenters from her, they left her alone in a cell.

Her father watched the nighttime broadcast in stunned disbelief. He couldn't believe that his sweet, gentle daughter had done something so rash. He pressed his gnarled fingers to his mouth as images of her face flashed across the screen. He had no idea the rage she had carried inside her. His own anger had burned down to ashes long ago. He shrugged back into his jacket and walked under the golden glow of streetlamps to city hall.

No one could tell him where his daughter was. There was no record of her or where she had gone. He was turned away politely the first three times. On the fourth day, armed guards escorted him down the pristine marble steps where Addie had unfurled her banner, forbidding him from asking again.

In a last effort, he traipsed back down to the Deep, as Addie had done a week prior. He knocked on Mrs. Martinez's splintered door, and was welcomed in. She gasped wetly for breath. Her skin had the telltale gray tinge of lung sickness. When he told her of what had happened to Addie, fat tears slid down her cheeks.

"But you should be proud," she said as she dried her face. "She's a very brave girl."

He wanted to feel pride. Instead, he felt hollow. He thanked Mrs. Martinez for her time and began his long trek home, heart aching. Addie had given him something he could not give her in return: safety, and a place among the Clouds.

After the first few weeks, Addie lost track of how long she'd spent in the prison. She wondered if it had done any good, spreading her message through the streets. She hoped her father could forgive her, even if he never understood why she'd done it. Over time, her face paled, regaining the ghostly pallor of her girlhood. Her days dragged on in monotony, devoid of sun, art, and companionship. Sometimes, Addie found her fingers curling delicately, as if embracing one of her pencils, the habit hard to shake. At night, she fell asleep with a soft smile upon her lips and dreamed of a sky stained with a kaleidoscope of color.

See Cidney Mayes's story "Visions for the Independent City of New York" online at Metaphorosis.
If you liked it, leave a comment. Authors love that!
Remember to subscribe to our e-mail updates so you'll know when new stories are posted.

About the story

I typically write my short fiction in 24-48 hours. If I am feeling very passionate about an idea, it's best for me to get as much onto paper as possible, even if that first draft is incredibly messy. My first foray into short fiction was through 48-hour contests, so I think my brain has been trained to operate in this way.

A lot of inspiration for this story comes from the housing crisis where I live in Portland, Maine. I have been increasingly struck by the sight of homeless encampments that have appeared, and continue to grow, here. Every few weeks, the city will break up the encampments and people will just move their tents to a different park or underpass. In contrast, more and more real estate is being built to attract wealthy buyers to sparkling waterfront properties. In a city of only 68,000, this disparity is shocking.

Expanding this polarity of socio-economic status into a giant city, set in the future, provided the foundation for this story. Addie is from the Deep, a place where her home is slowly being eaten away by rising seas, and the government doesn't really care about what happens to her or her neighbors. They're only concerned with aesthetics and in keeping up their idea of luxury, even though their wealth is literally built on the labor and lives of the people who live directly below them.

A question for the author

Q: If someone wanted to make an animated series out of your work, based on the title or recurring themes, what would it look like?

A: My favorite thing about this story is its setting. I envision the levels of this future New York City to have distinct designs, aesthetics, and color schemes. The Deep is dark and bleak, with steel ocean-gray tones. Old, rusted fire escapes create a lattice above the rotting buildings on this lower level, holding up the rest of the city. The Mids are an amalgamation of culture, color, and sound; much like present day New York. Though, they don't receive much natural light either. Their light comes from artificial sun lamps, and coveted real-estate is on the outer edges of the city where light can pierce the gloom. The Clouds, the upper level of the city where the wealthy and powerful reside, is a soft, airy place. Greco-Roman architecture, the best in new technology, salt-kissed breeze, and blinding sun abound. The clothes are sleek, soft-edged, and pale, much like wisps of clouds.

In an ideal world, the storyline for an animated series adaptation would focus on different characters who live here. Addie, the main character in this story, had one vision for New York; but this is a behemoth of a city. What would the lives of someone from the Mids or Clouds look like? How could their stories interweave to create a larger picture of the city and show how it evolved from the New York we know today into this one? In my mind, I have a lot of backstory on who governs the city, how they rose to power, and how they are battling not only the rising seas, but other power-hungry politicians as well as a populace on the brink of collapse.

About the author

Cidney Mayes is a middle school librarian from Portland, Maine with a passion for anything magical. When not writing, she enjoys giving tarot card readings, walking outdoors with a good audio book, or playing board games with her husband and friends.

cidneymayes.com,   X/Twitter: @CidneyMayes. Instagram: Cidney.mayes

The Final Face

Norah Lovelock

There were seventeen people left between Dia and the end of her commission.

Failed colonies were too expensive to run, difficult to maintain, and so her commission had sent her here to collect up the stragglers, put them into cryo, and take them back to the homeworlds. FC3-268b, dubbed Rija by the locals, was the last planet on her very long list. There were seventeen people left for her to collect.

And when it was over, she'd have to return to Central. She was old and damaged. She could make an educated enough guess: they'd decommission her.

Upload her memories to some storage somewhere and forget she ever existed: the fate of most custodians, useless until they weren't.

This colonist's house was away from the others. Against the general backdrop of neglect, it was stark in its upkeep. The front door was painted an obnoxiously bright yellow, the brickwork repaired instead of crumbling. Dead bushes wilted below its wide bay windows. Dia gave herself a moment. She was tired. She had done this thousands of times, yet it never grew easier. Then, finally, when she could wait no longer, she stepped close and knocked.

It took a minute before it opened. A pair of eyes squinted suspiciously at her from the narrow crack between the wood and frame. Then the stranger noted the ruins of Dia's faceplate, her torn plastic skin and exposed, stained circuitry, and said, conversationally, "You look like shit, don't you?"

Dia did look like shit. It had been a long time since she'd had maintenance beyond what she could do for herself. Working on planets several hundred lightyears away from Central did that to a robot. Her plastic skin had been torn by a particularly aggressive mammal on a desert planet, her faceplate ripped out by a colonist with a vendetta. Once, she might have been able to disguise herself as human—convince the humans, as immoral as it was, that she could understand their plight, making it easier to take them to the sleepship. Maybe— and the thought alone felt traitorous—she might've been able to run: find a nearby space station, hide herself among the humans, as innocuous and invisible as any of them. Maybe it was a childish dream. Sometimes, it felt like it was all she had.

But her visible circuitry betrayed her and there was no way for her to repair herself. She would have to wait until she returned to Central to see what they'd do to her.

"Thank you," she said dryly, inclining her head. The humans never greeted her warmly. "May I come in? I'm a custodian. I'm here to help."

After another moment of suspicious squinting, the woman pulled the door open wider and stepped aside. "All right."

The house was cluttered. The walls were filled with photos, competing for space against framed prints, children's drawings pinned into the drywall. Belongings filled every empty surface: magazines, crocheted pillowcases, blankets, coasters. Considering how beloved the woman appeared, it was fascinating that she lived here, alone in this big house, removed from the rest of the remaining colonists.

The woman led her through the chaos to an equally chaotic kitchen, where she sat at the table. After a moment of deliberation, Dia sat too.

"I'm Dia. What's your name?"

"Alma," the woman said, leaning forward, elbows on her thighs. "You here to convince me to leave, then? Homeworlds decided that Rija isn't worth supplying anymore?"

Dia immediately knew this was not a conversation she could win. Her spiel had been ready: her polite, well-practiced, 'I'm a custodian from Central. Due to cost-cutting measures, we're asking the residents of Rija to relocate back to the homeworlds via sleepship. You *can* choose to stay, but the food packets will stop, and you'll be disconnected from the network.' Alma had beaten her to the punch.

"No," she demurred. "I'm just wondering who'd want to stay behind."

Alma snorted. "Only ever known this place, haven't I?"

She'd heard that excuse hundreds—thousands—of times before. It was no longer compelling. "You are aware that Central will set you up on whichever of the homeworlds you'd prefer? That you'll be cut off from food packets and the network?"

"Of course. I don't want to leave, though. Not gonna pack all my stuff—" and, waving an expansive hand, it was clear she had a lot of it, "—into a suitcase for the sake of some mandate I didn't even choose."

Dia still asked the question, as rote as it had become: "Don't you have people who care about you? Friends who'll miss you if you stay behind?"

Alma scoffed. "Ain't no-one here who gives a damn about me."

It felt like a lie, but Dia didn't know enough to argue. She didn't want to argue. She wanted to leave. "I take it I won't be able to convince you."

"No," Alma said sharply. Then she paused, her lips twitching with sudden mirth, and added, "And anyway, I like the weather."

There wasn't any weather to like. Rija was a miserable planet. The buildings were grey; the scant vegetation was muted and dull. Only far out at sea did the planet gain colour: the deep green of algae, the planet's primary source of oxygen.

And here, beside the shuttle, the rest of the town was collapsing into the ocean. From afar, the tide was foam-tipped; closer, just below where Dia stood, the waves gnawed hungrily at the ruins of houses. Overhead, it was drizzling: fine, thin, terrible stuff that made her want to shield her ripped forehead with her hand to try and stop the water from reaching her electronics.

Trust her final assignment to be on a wet planet. With her broken faceplate, it was the last thing she needed.

"Hello?" a voice called. "Are you from Central?"

She turned. It was a family: three adults, an infant, huddled against the rain. Her processors sparked with recognition: she'd seen them on the info sent from Central. "We saw the shuttle," one of them said, his eyes roaming her face. "You've brought a sleepship, haven't you?"

"I have," she said gently. It was up in orbit, waiting for its final passengers. "You want to go up?"

They did.

Once the humans and their luggage were inside, Dia set the autopilot, leaned back in the pilot's seat, and watched out the window as the planet grew small beneath them.

Her thoughts drew back to Alma; Alma, who seemed so bizarrely possessive of this ugly, backwater planet. Sure, it had a breathable atmosphere, but that was hardly rare. Even from the sky it was monochrome. Only as they entered orbit did it gain beauty: the grey cut by great swathes of white cloud, the ocean revealed to be swirls of deep navy and dark green. She couldn't help her cynicism. The miracle of orbit could make anything beautiful.

And in orbit, too, was the sleepship, dignified against the backdrop of stars. In the back, the humans were talking, nervous but quiet. She'd be nervous too, if she were human.

Inside the sleepship, there were rows upon rows of cryopods: thousands of them, patiently waiting for the person inside to wake. She had recited her explanation so often that it no longer held meaning: each pod was a cryo system. It would freeze them but would feel like taking a very long and timeless nap, and when they woke up, they'd be in Central.

They were scared. They also couldn't go back now. When all were all settled, she sealed the pods. On her custodian node, she set the countdown and the commands; watched as the drugs kicked in, and, one by one, as they fell asleep. Eventually, the lights in their pods turned off. They began to freeze.

When she had first received this sleepship, she had been a different custodian with a different name. The ship had been empty. She'd been excited.

And now she'd sat through near a thousand cycles of travel, been to deserts and mountains, valleys and moons, and all she wanted now was to go back to Central. She didn't care if they decommissioned her; not anymore. She wanted this done. She wanted to rest.

Without any humans around, the room slipped into darkness to conserve energy. She didn't bother wishing them sweet dreams. They couldn't hear her anymore.

She took the shuttle back planet-side. There were just three families left: two bigger families and Alma. The thought of collecting them exhausted her, but the end was in sight.

According to the intel she'd been given via custodian node—and she did *not* envy whichever custodian had been tasked with reconnaissance—the families occupied a single row of houses, well-kept in comparison to the abandoned building. Despite the drizzle, she went on foot, angling her head down to try and keep her internal components dry.

Whoever had done recon had done a good job, because they were right. Three terraced houses huddled together against a long row, the front gardens overfull with exotic fauna: bright orange, luminous purple, stark in the gloom.

And Alma was outside. She was leaning against the doorframe, chatting to a man inside, her tone light and cheerful.

It was awfully coincidental that Alma had claimed no-one here liked her, yet here she was, conversational—warm. Then she turned and her expression narrowed. "Here to spirit this family away too, then?"

"No," Dia said, and pressed her hand against her still-attached forehead plate to try and shield the worst of the rain. "They went voluntarily."

"Only because you bullied them into it."

The man interjected with a valiant, "Alma! Don't be mean to it!", but it was clear Alma would not be deterred. She waved her hand at him, scowling. "Go look after the kids, Mailer. Tell 'em I'll give 'em electronics classes next week—if you're still here."

Dia wanted to retort with something sharp—that keeping them here would serve no purpose but their deaths; that Alma's determination to stay didn't grant her the right to trap everyone else here, too; that it certainly was strange that no-one cared for her, but she was giving electronics classes. Then the feeling faded. Arguing wouldn't help. It very rarely did.

Alma turned on her heel and began to make her way down the road. Dia paused —then, deciding Mailer was a future problem, followed. She fell into step. "Electronics classes?"

Alma shot her a sharp glance. "None of your business."

"I never suggested it was," she responded, purposefully mild. "You don't have to tell me anything you don't want to."

That earned her another sidelong glare —and then, after a moment of silence, a sigh. "A long time ago, I used to be a custodian technician."

A technician? They were rare to find outside of the Central homeworlds—near impossible to find on any of the planets Dia had ever been deployed to. Hope, sudden and terrible, rose in her chest. Maybe there were options beyond decommission. "You could replace my faceplate."

Alma stopped walking. She stared up at her, squinting through the rain, the droplets catching on her lashes. "Why d'you think I'd help you out?"

It felt so obvious to say it was nearly painful: "I need help, and you're the first technician I've encountered."

"Obviously," Alma grumbled. "I just dunno why you're coming to me. We're not friendly."

They weren't. But right now, that didn't matter, because Alma had something Dia needed—needed so desperately her electronics ached with it. "What do you want from me in exchange?"

"I don't want anything from you." She began to walk, expecting Dia to fall back into step, then said, tightly: "Fine. I'll do it. How bad's the damage on your internal circuitry?"

It was that easy? And she didn't even want anything in exchange? Dia spoke quickly before either of them could change their minds: "I can't smile properly, but I'm sure you've already noticed that. Anything else I wouldn't be too sure about."

"Thought you new models could self-diagnose?"

"I'm not a new model," she said wryly. "Can you do it or not?"

"Of course I can *do* it." Alma said it quickly, like it was a point of pride. She pushed open her front door, stepped inside, then turned to survey Dia properly: a long, slow look up and down. "All right. My workshop's in the basement, and it's drier down there than up here."

She had been expecting a small workshop —maybe enough for a single table, some spare parts. She hadn't been expecting a full workroom. There was a table in the centre for the custodian to lie on, whilst the walls were lined with shelves containing every part Dia knew she contained and then some.

Out here, so far from Central, there surely weren't enough custodians to warrant this level of set up. Rija was a backwater planet in a backwater system. While custodians were everywhere, there couldn't ever have been enough work to be able to make it into a *career.*

She turned to Alma, eyebrow raised. "You've been hiding this down here?"

"Not hiding," she retorted, but folded her arms and shifted her weight. "Everyone already knows. Kept up with it even after I retired." She looked back at Dia, then said, curt, "The face plates are up there. Choose one."

She did as instructed, depositing options on the table, trying to hide her delight. She could be whole once again. There were faces of every size and shape, colouring and structure: brown eyed, purple eyed; freckled or scarred or neither or both. With every face, potential opened before her. She plucked through them until one felt *right*: dark eyed and dark skinned, similar to the plastic skin on the rest of her body. "This one," she said, and pressed her finger to feel the way its— soon to be *her*—cheek compressed. She looked up at Alma. "Do I wanna know how you got it?"

Alma plucked it up in deft hands. "I bought it." Her fingers skated along its still cheek. Some deep tenderness shone through in her face, enough to wipe away her sullenness—but when she looked at Dia she was surly once more. "Do you want to power off? It'll be uncomfortable if you stay awake."

"I don't mind."

"Lie down," Alma instructed, and turned away to a metal chest of drawers to bring out her tools.

Dia lay. The table was cool against her back and neck, but not unpleasantly so. She couldn't see what Alma was doing, but she had been repaired enough to take a guess at what she could hear: Alma was pulling out a wheeled stool to perch on; the way the metal bolts and screws clinked against each other as she plucked them out of the drawers and into tiny bowls. She got out a drill and a set of screwdriver attachments, prepared a cotton swab and rubbing alcohol.

Finally, she was ready. Alma flicked on lights bright enough to blind a human. "Are you sure about this?"

Well, it wasn't like she could mess Dia's face up any further. She shut her eyes. "Yes."

Alma began by unscrewing something below Dia's chin, soft skin against her sensors—and then those same hands darted up, unscrewing something else near her temple. The touch was overwhelming, too fast for her to meaningfully process—fingers on the wires in her face, knuckles against the inside of her skull, and Dia knew she didn't need to breathe, but it left her breathless anyway: the terrible intimacy of it, this woman inside her, taking her apart.

Then, finally, a part of her face came away. She heard it hitting the little table next to her, metal and cold. Next, she knew, would come the specific servos to support the musculature of the face she'd once worn; the tiny processor that made it move.

She hadn't expected Alma to need to wriggle it out. Every careful nudge of those fingers felt like an earthquake. It left her tense, every fibre of her locked into stillness, Alma's knuckles warm against the inside of her face—that terrible face; the one she hated to have, hated to see, the touch burning like fire.

"Are you alright?" Alma asked, voice low. "I'm about halfway through. Do you need a break?"

"I'm fine," she said. Her voice, the traitor, didn't even quiver. "Are you okay to keep going?"

Alma paused. "Yes," she said finally, and the wriggling resumed.

Dia lay there and tried not to move; tried not to use her processor in thinking how Alma's hands were so hot inside of her, removing and discarding the parts of her that no longer functioned. And then, quite suddenly, it was too much: this room, the overhead lights, the feeling of someone poking at the exposed parts of herself. "I need a break," she breathed, and this time her voice shook.

"I'm almost done," Alma groused. She wriggled the processor sharply, and Dia stopped processing data entirely.

And then, finally, it came out, and Alma's hands withdrew, and Dia could *think* again. She sat up, jerking up without the excess weight of her broken faceplate, itching all deep inside like a wound she couldn't touch.

Alma didn't even have the grace to look at her. She was poking the ancient parts on the tray, turning them this way and that. "Hope I didn't ruin any of the prongs," she murmured to herself. She glanced up at Dia and, with characteristic brusqueness, said, "Lie down again. We're not done. Need to put the new one on."

Could Dia lie down? Could she tolerate even a moment more of that touch, so terribly invasive? She wasn't sure, but she had to. Walking around with no faceplate would be worse than a broken one. There would be no future for her at all. She forced her body back down onto the table and lay utterly still, not even letting her hands clench into fists.

But what had been difficult was now easy. She kept an eye on her internal chronometer as Alma worked, watching the minutes count down. Alma did the same in reverse to the new face: attached the processor, plugged in the circuit boards and servos, and made it align with the rest of her head. None of it took very long, even if Alma's hands were burning hot; even if Dia wanted, just a little, to crawl out of her own skin.

Slowly, hyperaware of her new eyelids, she opened her eyes to let them focus and unfocus. And finally, as Alma cleared off the finishing touches, Dia installed her new drivers.

Alma's hands drew away. The overhead light flickered off. "There," she said finally, quiet. "We're done."

Dia sat up. The weight of her new face was unfamiliar—heavier, but welcome. When she brought her hand up to touch, there was no longer the tangle of wires and circuits, but flesh—a little cooler than human temperature, but *hers*. Her nose; her lips.

"Want a mirror?"

"Please," Dia begged.

Alma held one up for her. If Dia had had a heart, it would've stopped—because it was her, Dia, but she wore a stranger's face. Unfamiliar, but not for long. She stared at herself and made faces, stretched her mouth and crinkled her nose in an attempt to remind herself that this was her, now. She checked the groove between her neckplate and faceplate and, if she hadn't known, wouldn't've been able to tell there was a seam at all.

Hope, sudden and terrible, rose in her chest. The suffering felt suddenly worth it, like she had gone through something terrible for something redemptive at the other side. And her discomfort hadn't entirely been Alma's fault. She could allow a little praise. "I'm not sure a Central technician could've done a better job."

"Thanks," Alma said, watching Dia's face. Then she turned away, putting away her tools, her shoulders a tense line.

Dia got to her feet. Even though she knew it may ruin the silent truce between them, she had to ask: "You really don't want to go with them?"

Alma didn't even turn to answer. "Go with them *where*? Some sterile homeworld? Where there's traffic and people and noise?" She snorted. "I'd rather stay here, thanks, even if that means dying."

It was human idiocy of the highest order; the derision, the belief she'd be fine even when Central would essentially starve her out. "Stay, then," Dia said, and took the stairs two at a time in leaving.

The man Alma had spoken to—Mailer—caught her on her way back to the shuttle. "Custodian," he barked.

He was heedless to her anger. "Yes?"

He paused, fixated on her new face for a split second before he said, "We're leaving. Network's been turned off, and I suppose we didn't realise what we were signing ourselves up for." He grimaced. Humans really did love to revel in their own misery. She wished she had that luxury. "All the rest of us are coming, apart from..."

"Yeah," Dia snarled. "I'm aware."

"We want her to come. It's convincing her that's the problem," he said, shrugging.

She knew what a good custodian would do. She would go back to Alma—explain to her, softly and patiently, that everyone else was leaving, and hope that it would jolt her into leaving too. Dia would point out that they did care about her. Maybe she'd even get Mailer's children to come along. She wasn't above emotional blackmail.

But Dia wasn't a particularly good custodian. She didn't want to face Alma's grumpy expression, her short words. She wasn't sure she had the patience. Some spiteful part of her wanted to leave Alma here; wanted her to stay here, alone, and understand just the choice she was making. But mostly it sounded like too much work.

"Alright," she said instead of something tight and unkind. "I'll take the rest of you up in the morning. You've got tonight to pack—to say goodbye."

He nodded. "Thanks." Maybe he meant it.

It rained that evening, hard and heavy. She sat in the shuttle and listened to it thunder on the roof. Once, she would've been forced to worry about the electronics in her face degrading. Now she didn't have to worry at all.

That didn't mean she was happy about it.

At least the colonist situation was improving. She'd be able to round them all up before her final due date—bar Alma, of course, who would stay unless Dia convinced her otherwise. And Alma *would* stay alone if she had to.

Her chronometer told her it was dawn when she heard a knock on the shuttle door. She slid it open to reveal the rest of the families, carrying suitcases and pet carry cages and whatever else they needed to bring with them. She ferried them up, settling them into their sleep pods, and they went easily—painlessly. She drank in the sight of them as they shut their eyes and dreamt of whatever world they'd wake up in.

And then, finally, she was alone, and Dia could put it off no longer.

She landed the shuttle near Alma's house—because now there was no need for politeness. The drizzle had stopped, the air thick and grey, and she walked through it and felt the rain smudge against her face, whole once more.

She could have knocked. She didn't bother. Instead, she pushed the yellow front door open, wiping her shoes on the mat, and stepped inside. "Alma?"

A low grumble, then: "I'm in the kitchen."

It was just as cluttered as her previous visits. No attempt had been made to clean —to bring away things Alma might want to transport with her. She was ferociously stacking plates, her shoulders drawn.

"I'm going," Dia said simply, "and I'm taking everyone else with me."

For a second Alma paused, and then her expression narrowed. She ever so carefully put down the plate, almost soundless, on the counter. Her voice was poisonous: "You don't understand."

It was an absurd, impossible claim. However old Alma was, Dia was far older. "At least I understand how short-sighted you are. You could teach the kids electronics classes anywhere—"

"Short-sighted?" Alma laughed unhappily. "No—really. It's you who doesn't understand." And she stepped forward and took Dia's hand in her own—and between them, a custodian node flared to life.

Dia froze. Data flickered through her, images layered upon images: Alma's deployment here, generations ago. Rija had swelled and swelled with more and more people who accepted her, universally, unilaterally, as human. How terrifying that had been. How wonderful.

And how she'd had to hide. How she'd been able to confide in only a few, but how that was rare; how she had learned to maintain her own faceplate, do her own updates, because otherwise someone would work it out—they'd tell Central, and she'd have to return to the hell that was custodian work. How she didn't want that. How she'd rather stay here, alone—rot and fade and disappear—than return to the purgatory of reality.

Or at least at first. How the days had become monotonous without something to structure them. How alone she was around humans, hiding amongst them, unable to relate to them; unable to have them relate to her in turn.

Dia's broken face at Alma's front door, and Alma's terror at knowing she was going to be taken back to Central.

Dia staggered away. She knew it was programming—knew it was the facsimile of some human emotion—but her knees felt weak with sudden, terrible understanding. "You're not—"

"No," Alma said, and her anger had faded to something quiet, something sad. "I'm not."

She could see no evidence of a seam or seal in Alma's earnest face, although that was the point of them, wasn't it? It was what Dia herself had delighted in scant hours before: that if you didn't already know, there would be no way to tell they were anything other than human.

"I've maintained myself as best possible with a single pair of hands," Alma continued. "And when I saw you—I thought the ruse was up. Thought it was all over; that you were here to take me back to Central."

"No. I doubt Central even knows you're here. I thought you were just another human." Her words stumbled out, unwieldy in the wake of her understanding: "I mean, now I know, I can leave you here..."

But Alma shook her head. "I'm tired of this: of hiding from Central, of being on a backwater planet, living in fear, being lonely. I don't want to be this person anymore."

Dia didn't say anything. She was tired in a similar way: tired of being the good custodian.

"What do you want to do?" Alma asked. "Because with a second pair of hands, you could change your faceplate too. You wouldn't have to be a custodian anymore. You could disguise yourself as human— could be anyone you wanted."

It was nothing she hadn't thought of before—but somehow Alma saying it made it sound impossible, a reality she'd never be able to achieve. She knew what she wanted. She could feel hope surging up inside her, fragile and tentative. She just didn't know whether it was justified. "What do *you* want to do?"

Alma paused, then said, "I want you to ask the question you need to ask."

It was enough to make Dia fumble, almost forgetting the point of all this: "Will you come up to the sleepship?"

"Now I know you're not going to tell Central about me... of course," Alma responded, and smiled.

The flight that had seemed so boring gained an odd magic with Alma as a passenger. Dia set the autopilot and together they stared out the window. They watched as the ground gave way to the town, then the jut between land and ocean, and finally just cloud cover, Rija no more than a sphere hanging, weightless, in the infinite dark.

"You alright?" Dia asked softly.

"Fine," Alma said, nodding jerkily. "What happens when we get up there?"

"I... don't know."

"Dia," she said, and her voice was heavy—weighted. "I notice you didn't answer my question. What do *you* want to do?"

The shuttle thrummed as it piloted itself into the sleepship. What did she want to do? More than anything, she wanted to be honest. "I... don't want to be a custodian anymore." Saying it aloud was terrible, a truth that felt awful to admit, yet her relief was stronger. "I don't know what else I can do, but... I don't want to go back to Central." She didn't want to be uploaded onto some databank somewhere, forgotten about, her memories rendered into files.

Alma's smile was small and warm, and enough to make Dia surge with sudden, desperate hope. "With two of us, we don't have to go back to Central. Being alone and scared was what made me stay. But we could—"

"We *could* leave," Dia interrupted, her hope turning from a trickle into a waterfall. "We could repair each other; cover for each other. I wouldn't have to do this anymore. You wouldn't have to hide on some backwater planet in case Central comes looking." It was like an invisible weight was being removed from her shoulders: she wouldn't have to carry the burden of these people; of their frustration and joy. She'd done her job as best she was able. She hadn't let anyone down.

And, most importantly, with Alma's help, she could leave.

"We should take them most of the way," Dia added. "The humans. Let's find a planet—a station, even—and set the autopilot to take the humans back to Central. Then we can run." They could hide among the humans, invisible among them. They'd have to be careful, but careful was better than decommissioned.

Alma was still grinning. "Yeah. Alright, then," she said, like it was easy. "Think I can live with that."

Dia knew she didn't have a stomach—just metal and wires—but it flipped anyway. Together, they could be anyone. They'd have to hide from Central, would never be able to stay anywhere long... but she'd been doing that for a long time under their orders. She'd rather do them under her own.

Around them, the shuttle fell to silence. Then Dia took a deep, unnecessary breath. The universe was unfurling before her, every possibility suddenly within reach. She'd collected the other sixteen people from Rija. The seventeenth was offering her something she hadn't even dared to dream of: an escape from oblivion.

"Okay," she said, smiling back, wide enough that it near ached: "Yes. Okay. Let's do it. Let's see what's out there."

See Norah Lovelock's story "The Final Face" online at Metaphorosis.
If you liked it, leave a comment. Authors love that!
Remember to subscribe to our e-mail updates so you'll know when new stories are posted.

About the story

"The Final Face" originated from a question I had about a lot of sci-fi: if there are all these people going in and out of cryo-freeze all the time, who's the person putting them there? I then decided it would have to be someone; asking people to voluntarily do something without any external pressure or help is generally a recipe for disaster. I decided she'd have to be a robot, as she would therefore not be susceptible to being frozen herself, but she'd have to look and behave human enough that humans would be able to trust her—and that's where Dia, the narrator, was formed.

I quickly also realised that she needed something to be in opposition to; it wouldn't be a story if she just put people into cryofreeze without anything to rally against! That was how Alma came into being.

Fundamentally, for them both, I was very interested in writing about the idea of them looking and behaving in very human ways—and yet, despite that, being indefinably "non-human" in some way that is impossible to remedy. Alma can disguise herself as human, but for Dia, the task is impossible. Even when returned to a human appearance, the colonists see her as other, a label that's impossible for her to escape.

Setting-wise, I was heavily inspired by the Atlantic Coast of Ireland. Although I love to live in cities, I enjoy writing about isolated natural environments. I found the very stark, grey ocean very beautiful—and very cold to swim in!

A question for the author

Q: What inspires you?

A: People! I'm a character-driven writer and like to imagine how people might behave in imagined futures. I don't think we'll change much!

Generally, my ideas come from building a character (or characters) in my head before working out what kind of situation that character may be in and generally run from there. Sometimes these characters appear fully formed, but more often than not it involves piecemealing traits together: that person I spoke to the other day who told me about their partner, that character from another piece of media I really enjoyed, a personal experience that I'd like to write about... Ultimately, I'm a writer who is most interested in and inspired by character and people above all else.

About the author

Norah Lovelock is a speculative fic writer from Manchester, UK.

https://norah.love

When Darkness Falls on Edinburgh

C.J. Erick

It was Gavina's favorite image of Edinburgh: the spire of the gothic Scott Monument rising above the skyline of rainbow-colored shop fronts on Victoria Street, with the setting sun lighting the monument's peak in golden fire. The colored shop facades marked Thomas Hamilton's redesign of the original Bow Street in colorful Flemish sensibilities, the renaming when the queen ascended the throne in 1837, and a salute to gay pride. Or, for Gavina, white light manifested as a spectrum by the faceted glass of an aged oil lantern.

Walking down the curving narrow street was like walking backwards in time, perhaps to the era of the witch burnings. The smells of food and wet stone, sounds of hawkers and music, and light dazzling in the mist were spectra for the senses. Moist air oddly blowing from the south brought mist, pale as her translucent skin where it peeked from beneath her dark cloak. Her pale skin spoke of delicacy, fragility, something precious. She hated her skin sometimes.

Victoria Street led to Forrest then High Street. She paused there, looking west toward the Castle. The brownstone buildings on each side of the street were like hands reaching up, with shops like bracelets around their wrists. In the valley of their open palms sat Edinburgh Castle, lit to golden red by electric lights, the turbulent deep turquoise and gray sky above it like ocean water. One expected great fish and whales and mythical creatures, perhaps selkies, to swim in great grand circles above and around it.

She reached the shop, hers now, an old one, hardly noticeable among all the other tourist traps along this street. The sign above the door was faded just to the appropriate shade of ambiguity: Miss Aileen's Mysteries and Potions.

Suddenly, she felt tired, as if gravity was pulling her into a smaller, squatter version of herself.

Gods mighty and fay, I miss you, Aila. We need you now more than ever.

Dusk was giving way to night when she unlocked the door with the old skeleton key, which seemed to warm when it found its home in the old brass lock. The only light in the shop was coming from an old Oban whisky sign on one wall, the one Captain Petr refused to throw out. The light was good, though. It kept her from barking her thin shins on the displays and counters as she wended her way back to the old office.

Petr was there, even though she'd told him to take a few days off to enjoy fishing or hiking. He missed the Highlands like the raven he was. But he was a lovable raven, one with a snaggled beard and feathery hair grayed by more age than he would admit. At times, one might see a shadow clinging to him as if he were a spirit afoot. Darkness took no pity on the poor man, Aileen had said, which was his punishment for defying it.

Petr sat hunched at their big wooden desk, snoozing over a leather-bound book older than he was, probably. She picked up his plate with breadcrumbs and bits of cheese and the glass with dribbles of milk, and took them to the tiny kitchen at the back of the shop. Not much of one, really, just an old one-burner gas range with an oven too small for even a loaf of soda bread, a sink too small for a decent-sized pot, and a tiny, grungy window that looked out on the alley behind it.

When she returned to the little alcove they called the office, he'd awakened and poured himself a short glass of brown, oily liquor — whisky, reeking like a bale of wet peat. He offered her the bottle, but she declined. She fancied a wee dram now and then, but not at the moment, not with so much on her mind.

She slumped into the wooden rolling chair opposite his, the one worn smooth by decades of polishing by Aileen's self-proclaimed iron butt. Like the door lock, it always seemed warmer than expected. The captain pushed the old book he'd been reading across to her. The black leather cover was worn at the edges, but otherwise well-kept.

"What's this?" she asked.

"Something the lady wanted me to give you. At the right time."

"Right time? For what?"

"I dunno, lass. Maybe it will become apparent after you have a look."

The book looked sturdy and heavy enough, but she felt it might explode into black and yellow dust if mishandled. Inside the front cover lay sheets of folded paper, newer than the book, a few years old at most. She unfolded them and found words in Aileen's hand, two pages, one a few lines of verse and the other a personal note addressed to her. She felt a quiver.

"How long have you had this book, Petr?"

"Long enough. And that's all I'll say about it."

"Why didn't you give it sooner? Like three months ago when she passed?"

"Like I said, Gavina, the lady told me to give it to ya when the time was right. She said I'd know when. She was right. And you know it too, don't you, lass?"

"I don't know what you mean."

"Yes, you do."

Yes, damn him, she knew. Look for the chill wind coming from the south and not the north as it should. Watch for flocks of dark birds riding high in the evening wind. Feel the tremor in the earth like a deep growl rising from the bowels of it. She'd noted all these things in recent weeks, but the wind was an odd, late season cyclone. The birds were flocks starving after fires on the mainland of Europe, crossing the Channel in search of food. And the vibrations she felt — construction work around the palace, rollers and shovels and cranes moving large sections and blocks. Nothing unnatural in any of that, all explained by known things.

"The signs will always seem to be usual, Gavina," Aileen had said. "The ominous will always be hidden in common things."

"She said you must read the notes," prompted Petr.

She slipped the pages out of the book, unfolded them and pressed them flat on the desktop. But to read Aileen's words would bring the heartache, resurrect the pain that had plagued Gavina in the hard weeks since she and Petr had held Aileen's hands where she sat in the big upholstered chair, where she'd insisted they place her. They'd watched Aileen's slowly shallowing last breaths.

Gavina chose to read the letter first. Aileen's writing was still strong and straight. Not the hand of a woman dying of cancer.

Dear Gavina:

I must start by saying I am sorry. I hoped to deal with the coming storm myself, but it was not to be, and I must think this is the way the gods wanted it. My powers, once strong, are now weak, too weak, and so my time as the guardian has come and gone. I would not have it this way. I would not force this great responsibility on someone as young and bright and full of potential and promise as you, but...

Here, Gavina imagined Aileen pausing and trying to find the best words, perhaps wiping a single tear away, full of memories of love and conflict and sorrow that she'd rarely spoken of, even to her ward and mentee Gavina, whom she treated like her own daughter.

...this decision is not mine to make. You came to me by providence because you are the chosen, and there is nothing you or I can do about that. May the gods lay their miserable and spiteful eyes upon you with mercy.

Evil comes in many forms, and likewise the ones chosen to fight it. Our way is the rare way, the light of night. For we walk in the shadowy streets and wait for when we are needed. That time is again upon our land, and so upon you, my lovely girl. We are the way of the lantern, the glass, the burning wick. But we are also connected to the Earth, as those who come are, those who come to claim that which is not theirs.

They will come as three, the children of my foe, Madame Griselda. Trust not their youthful smiles. Griselda and I were sisters once, in the Coven at North Berwick, along with Petr, whose time in merchant marine was past. But the Satanic Panic in the 1980's forced us to disband, and left Griselda bitter. She called me a fool of the light. This sentiment she will have passed on to her children. They will regard you coldly.

Be brave, lovely girl, for you know within yourself where your strength lies. Your enemies are powerful, but you are greater.

Be brave. I will be with you.

Love,

Aileen

Aileen had spoken often of the gods she believed in, the evils that fought for chaos, the followers of the Gaelic devil, Black Donald, in his quest to corrupt all the peoples and cover the land in ash and dark snow. She'd spoken of the power of the lantern and the glowing coals, the mirror and the prism and the faceted glass. These were all magical things, she had said, and beyond Black Donald's power to corrupt.

But was any of it still powerful in the modern world?

So Griselda had taken to the dark side alone, pushing away the way of light, forsaking duality and balance. When freedom and respect could not be achieved through cooperation and service to the people, it would be wrenched from the hands of non-believers via force.

Petr was watching Gavina now, his brows knitted and eyes pinched. He didn't speak much of the anti-paganism he and Aileen had endured as they fled the mob from North Berwick, but Aileen had hinted at his bravery. How easy it would have been for he and Aileen to follow the way of darkness, as Griselda had.

Gavina took the second sheet of paper, the one with the verse, and spread it before her. The words were Gaelic, and she struggled to translate them.

*Chan eil dorchadas an taobh eile de
sholas; tha e dad.
Chan eil an taobh eile den dorchadas
aotrom; tha e a h-uile dad.
Nuair a bhios solas agus dorchadas a
'tighinn còmhla, faodaidh a' bhuil a bhith
mar rud sam bith.*

"I can't read this, Petr."

He took the sheet from her, his eyebrows rising.

"It's an old one, Gav, something spoken even before the Druids walked the lands to the north, before the pagans built their mystic stone observatories.

*"The opposite of light is not darkness; it is nothing.
"The opposite of darkness is not light; it is everything.
"When light and darkness converge, the consequence can be anything."*

He handed the paper back to her.

"I don't understand it, Petr. A Book of Genesis reference? But the last line..."

"I could guess, but that would be of little help to you. You must seek your own meaning. Aileen gave this to you for these times, so your understanding is important."

"What could be coming? When she spoke of the dark times in the past, her words were always allegorical and inscrutable. Things about the children of the deep earth and forest, the creatures of the night, the spirits of the shadows — crazy talk. Weren't they just silly tales meant to keep the children in line, not real-world evil?"

"There isn't any difference. The stuff of nightmares speaks of real evil."

She reread the verse.

"It's just a puzzle, an enigma. 'The consequence can be anything.' Something outside the real world, like dividing by zero? Or that old saw about an unstoppable force striking an immovable object? What is infinity divided by infinity?"

"Nothing. Everything. Or perhaps just... one."

His hands raised from a sketch he'd been fiddling with while he listened to her ranting, a doodle. She recognized it as the Celtic quaternary knot, infinite loops forming four points. It represented many things: the four primary directions; the four elements of nature; the four seasons;

or the four Wiccan sabbats, the fire festivals. The last of them, Samhain, was three days away. Some called it Halloween.

Samhain marked the end of the season of light and the beginning of winter, the season of darkness. In that transition, the veil that separated the physical world with the spirit world faded to ethereal thinness. In that time, the spirits, both good and evil, might leave the spirit world and walk the earth again.

Fia cast the stones on the gray tile board, careful to keep them on the surface. Stones that left the board might fall either way, toward power or weakness, like smoke drifting from a wisping pipe or smudge-burning sage. Better to remove uncertainty and control all that was within one's grasp. That had always been Griselda's advice.

She studied the six pieces, each one a different shape, size, number of facets, shades of gray and black. There was a pattern, and a surprise, a good one.

"The woman is truly dead," she said. "The stones confirm it."

Mairi, sitting opposite her at the table, lifted her thick black brows. Dorn, whose full name was Dorn Dubh, Black Fist, hardly moved from where he sat on their one sofa, staring at his hands. They were very different, the three of them. How could they have crawled from the same womb within minutes of each other? Fia, as the first born, had become their leader, by ancient covenant.

Fia added, "She is childless."

"Then it's done," said Dorn. He stood, leaving a depression in the dark red leather. He moved about the room in a slow-motion dance, touching things; the dark shade of a brass lamp that cast its light only downwards, tinted glass jars of minerals and ground bone, a wide book of ancient maps with its charcoal leather cover turned open to one they'd been surveying for the three months since Griselda's death, the map of inner Edinburgh, the city fifty miles away from their remote, little-known castle, the place that was the subject of their thoughts every day since Griselda had wheezed her last malodorous breath and cursed them to bring the night down at last.

"Why do I still feel tension?" said Mairi. Mairi — The One Who Is Bitter. Bitter at being the youngest? "I feel the woman's powers still present."

"Nonsense," said Dorn. "If the old hag's dead, her powers died with her. The time is now ours to claim Castle Hill as the witches' hallows, and all the death-shrine that lies in the bloody soil beneath it. Hundreds died there because of people's fearful hatred. It's all ours now. The witches will reign." He used the Gaelic word for witches, buidsichean.

Fia felt her sister's bitterness, like the darkest of chocolates, burnt blacker than black. She also felt her brother's excitement, his lust for the power that had so long been denied her kind, the promises of the dark angel, Black Donald. He was the Breaker, destroyer of the non-Wiccan, builder of the dark age that was to come, fulfillment of the prophecies. When the power of the deepest earth would rise to sweep over the land like the wings of a great dark bird.

Three days until Samhain, November 1. One of the four fire festivals, and the most powerful, the beginning of winter. The dark winter they had all dreamed of as the followers of Griselda, The One Who Dwells in a Gray Castle. Their mother.

Gavina slept little for the following three days. She ran the shop during the four evening hours it was open, to maintain the routine, to keep curious eyes from gazing too deeply through the windows and into the shop's shadows. And of course to keep them fed. But all night and into the morning, she pored over the books of handwritten notes and observations, verses and incantations, everything Aileen had guided her with, spoken of, made her practice. She still didn't know whether most of it held any real power or, even if it did, whether she knew how to invoke it.

She was deeply lost in the special book Petr had given her days before, the thick, leather-bound volume of special quotes and verses, each one meant for a different day.

The verse for Halloween read this in ancient Gaelic, which Petr had translated:

As the hours fall
So shall the veil
The dead and wicked will walk
And the two worlds shall be one.

Until light breaks in the east
And the spirits must rest again.

Petr cleared his throat behind her, breaking her mood, so unearthly quiet when he wanted to be. He reached around her and turned the book's cover closed.

"This will do you no more good tonight, girl."

"Then what will, elder? All of this —" She waved her hand toward the piles of books, scrolls, notebooks, and envelopes big and small, all old. "I don't know what I could need and what's just a waste of time. I don't even know the enemy."

"Yes, you do. The enemy is darkness, all those things you are not."

"It's dark now. Is the night our enemy?"

"Not now, but it could be. I'm not talking about the time between sundown and sunup. I'm talking about the eternal darkness that rises from the world, not that which falls from the sky."

"Then how will I know it? How will I fight it?"

"What did your friend and patron call you, when you were morose or when you needed a good chastising to take this all seriously?"

Gavina couldn't answer for a moment. When she did, her voice was tight and brittle.

"Gavina, of course. Little White Hawk."

"That's your spoken name. Its meaning comes in the day, when you're challenged by the physical world. What did she call you when you were challenged by the ethereal?"

"Lantern Girl."

"Yes."

"It always felt silly, like she was making fun of me."

"Think on her name. What does it mean in the physical world?"

"Aileen. Ray of Sunshine."

"Aye. Not many were brighter than she, Gavy. Do you know her spirit name?"

"No. She never spoke of it to me."

"But you know it. The same as yours, at least when she was young. Lantern Girl. A title passed down from olden times. She didn't choose your spirit name by chance or whim. When she found you with the homeless urchins, lighting trashcan fires for the bums, she recognized your way. You are the way of the wick, the burning flame, the faceted glass, the light which guides carriages and ships and people through the night, through the underground.”

“I don't feel that.”

“You will when you need to.”

“I feel something, a shadow, like a black hemorrhage coming over the land. And I don't know how I can feel it.”

“What you need now is rest. Get some sleep, Gavina. Darkness is not evil in itself. All living things need it, for renewal. Just as you do.”

“But there's no time. I don't know what we're facing, or how to prepare.”

Petr said nothing for a moment, measuring his words.

“Gavina, you are the way of fire, not the fire that burns and destroys, but the fire that lights the way and enlightens the soul. You are the way of the lantern, the glowing ember, the fire that warms and heals. Did you think Aileen found you by chance? Nay. She was drawn to you as a kindred spirit. You are both the way of the lantern, the vessel of fire one may carry. And that's the weapon you must wield.”

He urged her to her feet and guided her toward the sleeping area in the back of the shop. But her mind refused to rest, roiling with images and fears so that she didn't know if she slept or merely lay awake with her eyes closed, haunted by visions.

Dorn led his siblings up the rising streets toward Edinburgh Castle, leaping ahead of his sisters as he had done when they were younger, usually to Fia's annoyance. Age and cynicism had molded him into the snarling young man he'd become in their isolation in the old castle, a more demonstrative counter to Mairi's quiet moroseness. His unbridled enthusiasm seemed to have returned. Beside Fia, Mairi seemed if anything even quieter. But even in her, the spark of adventure and anticipation had come to life, like a tiny struck match.

It was late afternoon, cloudy, dead calm in the street, almost stale, but strong winds high up, driving the mottled gray and indigo clouds. October 31; Halloween to the laypeople, who totally missed the true meaning, the fire festival, disrespected as a barely remembered pagan event. High Street was populated, more than the last time Fia had walked it, six years earlier. When her mother had dared to bring her, just the two of them, leaving Dorn and Mairi with a school acquaintance in Aberdeenshire.

Griselda's words echoed in her head:

"The Castle Hill, Fia. That's where you'll make your stand. The blood and power of all those who were unjustly murdered there remain. It is time for the children of darkness to take back that power, and to take the land to where it was always meant to be. Time for the influence of those of us who see a better future, to overcome the fools who only see the naïve innocence of lightness."

Students moved around the street, primer age in white and black uniforms, no tribal tartan allowed. Older higher school boys and girls, itching in their skins to become adults, wore everything and sometimes nearly nothing, some already in costumes, many of haunted things or demons, some absurdly in those of celebrities or food items or political characters from the news, but some in dark goth clothing that made Fia laugh. The gay human enthusiasm for the pagan holiday, these would-be Wiccans, or followers of some other order they knew nothing about. The need to identify themselves as different, outside the norms of proper society. *Oh, be patient, young souls, your time will come, so soon now. That which is odd will become common. Those who are outcasts will rule.*

So comforting that all the tools she and her siblings needed were in their trendy red and black shoulder bags, easy to bring to this place without suspicion. Their gray and black clothing blended in well with the students, even the older ones, the university gems, who thought the world revolved around them even more now than when they were primer age. Perhaps Fia, Dorn, and Mairi should just leave everything as it was so these pretentious elitists could find out how little the world cared about them.

They worked their way west, uphill, climbing the cobblestones past the tourist shops. At the corner of Forest, Fia paused. Something felt strange there, like business left undone, like an oven left burning or letters unsent. Dorn was halfway up the next block before he realized she'd stopped. He loitered where he was, didn't return to where she stood. Annoyed, she gathered Mairi, who'd stopped to watch her from the doorway of a bookseller, looking unperturbed.

"I thought we were in a hurry," said Dorn, when she and Mairi reached him. "Were you looking to hail a cab?"

"I felt something disturbing, black head," Fia said, using the Gaelic, ceann dubh. The old language was creeping into her speech more and more, as if she were channeling her mother and her kin. "We're not alone here."

He huffed. "With the woman dead, no one else matters now. The grounds are ours for the taking."

"It's not the grounds I'm concerned about. It's the very Earth. And arrogant complacency is a danger we cannot afford." She paused to listen and feel, but she felt nothing and heard nothing beyond the sounds of people and traffic and the rising wind in the high wires and towers. Even the light from the castle seemed subdued, as if expecting them. "Maybe I'm overreacting. But let's prepare our things as soon as we can."

They entered the open yard leading into the main entrance to the castle, the esplanade, where the annual Fringe Festival was held. The thought of dozens of traditional and modern bands playing there and tens of thousands of sweating people in that small slanted concrete platform made her skin crawl.

Mairi cast a cloak of mist and shadow over them, and they passed the gates just before the castle was closed for the evening. The landmark workers and the real soldiers walked by them without notice, as if they were invisible spirits. Though they weren't of the spirit realm, after this night they might live for ages, the guardians of the damned souls who had been murdered here. So many witches and innocent laypeople had been caught in mob hysteria that descended on this place.

May it all be made right in the night, and in the many days of blessed darkness that will follow.

They walked around the winding walled streets of the castle, up past the parade stages, around the tabernacle and hall of heroes, to the highest observation lane, the best vantage point over the city. Ancient black cannons pointed outward at the sea, the land, the forests below, and toward Arthur's Seat, the hill in Holyrood Park, another site of witch burning. They were surrounded by places of power the spirits would occupy over the days ahead.

Mairi laid her pack down, withdrew a small stone pot the size of a grapefruit, and filled it with herbs and organic matter. She cast a spell of protection and isolation, warding off any of the night guard from coming to this high, stone-walled avenue. This was her work for the night, to keep her pot smoldering with the pungent leaves and bracken and moldy peat while Fia and Dorn cast bigger things. When her incantation was complete, she settled onto a seat on the high wall where she could watch them.

Dorn swung his pack down and removed six black-glazed bricks, cut into twelve halves on their long flat sides. He laid these in a circle about a half-meter across. In this he laid short rods of stainless steel he'd made for this occasion. The rods formed a grating in the bottom of the brick circle. He placed pieces of kindling from his pack on the grate, along with some paper as starter, and lit it with a red plastic wand lighter. With all of this, the pack had weighed three or four stone. But Dorn had the strength of the earth behind him and had carried it as one might a pack of duck feathers.

Dorn represented the earth, Mairi the restless sea, and Fia the sky. And now they had applied the flame to wood — fire, the fourth element. The circle of physical and ethereal energies was complete.

Fia laid her pack near the expanding fire, taking in the pleasant smells of burning wood. She could feel the terror of the ones burned at the pyre on the flat ground just over the wall far below them, hear their cries and wailing, hear their flesh and hair sizzle, smell the stench. Anger rose within her, but she held it in check. In anger was rashness, and she needed a cool head. The darkness was not emotional; it was calm and relentless, and so must she be as well.

She drew leather pouches from her pack, thirteen in all, herbs and bones and insect hives and the skin of reptiles. These things were not magical in themselves, but in the things they represented, the magic that had been ingrained in them by Fia's mother, and her parents and grandparents before her. The items were hundreds of years old, some of them irreplaceable. Some Griselda had brewed, others Fia and Mairi had concocted from the old journals, exactly as had been done generations before by those who had never seen ships and cars and television and the computer age. Had the world been a better place back then when things were simpler, as Griselda had lamented?

Fia added these things to the fire in the order Griselda had taught, reciting the learned words. One by one, the ingredients of the eternal darkness, the endless winter, charred and burned in the low flames, sending gray and green smoke upward into the darkening sky, up toward the flying clouds. Yet the smoke did not blow away in the wind, but rose as if in its own invisible chimney toward the sky.

As she added the last ingredient, the smoke paused for a few seconds, the air seemed to halt its elemental motion, and Fia couldn't breathe. Dorn's eyes widened and his mouth opened and closed like a fish's or like a clenching fist. And then the moment passed and the smoke doubled, dark and beautiful, like the mane of a mighty black horse. It rose in a twisting column up to the flying clouds, and then turned into an eerie mist, rolling back down over the city. This blanket of gray mist flowed from the castle, following the streets like coiling snakes.

There was little to do but watch and wait, for the dark fog to complete its consumption, for the veil between the worlds to dissolve for the night, for the real work to begin, the building of a new time, a new world.

But the fog had concealed the approach of another, the presence she'd sensed as they'd walked up High Street. From the lower part of the castle, two figures came up the stoned street, both dressed in dark hooded jackets and dark clothing. One was a hulking form, bent over probably from age, face hidden. The other was smaller, about Fia's size. They walked to where Fia and her siblings waited, all watching them now.

The two set down their own backpacks, red and black leather, the best colors to hide at night. The small one pushed back its hood and revealed a young woman no older than Fia, with dark hair and moon-pale skin. Her huge eyes were haunting, like an owl's or hawk's. Fia felt she knew this woman, even though she had never seen her before.

"You're the old woman's daughter," Fia said.

The woman seemed taken aback by that, as if this were something she had never considered. The bigger figure pushed back its hood, revealing a gray-haired man with a wide forehead bent like his back, and small eyes dancing with blue fire.

The strange woman gazed at the sky. The blackness from the sea had crossed halfway now, engulfing the circle of darkness from the fire smoke. Dorn ignored the woman and her elder companion and added more wood. Mairi sat on the wall and kicked her feet. Her little pot continued to sizzle, although the need for it seemed to have come to an end.

"Very nice," said the young woman, continuing to gaze upward.

"I'm glad you like it." So ludicrous that this one would come now, when it was far too late for an intervention. The elder man waited beside her, like a trite legend. "I'm Fia. And your name?"

"Gavina." Her own name sounded strange in her ears.

Below the castle, the people of Edinburgh didn't realize something very wrong was happening in the sky, that the darkness falling was more than just a heavy cloud layer moving over the setting sun. Random sirens twee-dee'd below, but in no greater number than a normal holiday evening. Across the expanse of foggy air, crowds were gathering on top of Arthur's Seat. Not the safest place to be, probably.

"Gavina? Hmm. The White Hawk," said the young woman who'd called herself Fia, which meant Dark Peace. That name brought a fresh chill to the air. "Are you the old woman's daughter?"

A pang, not heavy or deep, but sharp.

"No."

"She is," said Petr. "By any measure that matters."

"And you are?" asked the young man, who'd stepped forward.

"Your nightmare," said Petr, meeting his eyes coolly.

"My brother, Dorn," said Fia, "and this is our sister, Mairi."

"The Fist and the Bitter One," said Petr. "Appropriate."

"Well, this has been *so* nice," said Fia, "but as you can see, we're rather busy. Why are you here?" Her eyes flashed with malice.

Gavina removed from her pack a small metal lantern as tall as her outstretched fingers, with straight glass sides set in a hexagonal shape. Then she took out a white paint pen and hesitated over the side of the lantern.

"Which one, Petr?" she asked.

Petr eyed the three young people marveling at them.

"Make it the triquetra. There is worthy power in that one."

The triquetra, symbol of interwoven trinity, of body, mind, and spirit, or the elements of land, sea, and air, or the three stages of life; child, adult, elder.

She nodded and drew a simple Celtic knot with three points on the metal base of the lamp. The pagan symbol shone boldly white against the dull gray steel of the lantern and seemed to sparkle with its own internal energy. Such ancient beauty in it, and hidden power. Next, she pulled a lighter from her pocket, chanted quietly, lit the lantern, and set it on the stone at her feet. Immediately, it flared, pushing white light from the lamp, brighter and brighter. Resting on the stone, it resembled a model lighthouse from a child's electric train set.

The light expanded in a bubble of clean air, wider and wider, pushing wisps of dark fog away from the castle street.

Fia's brow furrowed in dark shadows. "Dorn, crush that thing."

Dorn stepped forward and stomped the lantern, leaving it a tiny hulk of metal and broken glass. The flame sputtered and died, and the wisps of fog reappeared.

"That wasn't it," said Gavina. She took an identical lantern from her pack. "Maybe the triskele?"

"Worth a try," said Petr.

Dorn stepped forward to seize the new lamp, but Fia stayed him with a gesture. "Let her try again. This amuses me."

Gavina drew a design with three spiral swirls connected to a central hub, then lit the lantern and set it on the pavement. The triskele, another symbol of trinity, this one associated with movement, a moving forward, a hope that it would touch the three foes before her with light and enlightenment. Again, the flame came up and brightened, and the dark fog cleared away. Again, Dorn stepped forward and crushed the lantern with his heavy black boot. The flame died, and the fog returned.

"Nope," said Gavina. "What next?"

"We tire of this game, White Hawk," said Fia. "The time for your ways is gone, and our time is here. Dorn, see them out."

"Gladly." He stepped toward Gavina.

"Not a good idea," said Petr, not moving from where he stood at Gavina's side.

"Get out, old man. You're moving on. We'll let you live in a dank old castle out in the fen somewhere."

He seized Petr's elbow and shoulder and shoved, but there was hidden power in Petr he hadn't counted on. They struggled and grappled, but the younger man was the stronger and moved Petr back down the street toward the castle entrance.

"I'd hate to kill another witch on these haunted grounds," Dorn said, "but I'll throw you over the wall, I swear it."

Petr leaned away, pulled a dark device from his pocket, and pointed it at Dorn. There was a harsh electric buzz, and Dorn staggered back, fell to the ground, and rocked in tremors. A Taser. Petr had not told Gavina about that.

Petr said, "Remember, young 'un, old age and treachery beat youth and skill."

Gavina pulled another small lantern from her pack.

"You're wasting your time, little bird," said Fia. "Your weak powers are nothing, even if we don't destroy your little matchlights."

"Three of you, for the basic elements, correct?" said Gavina. "Let me guess. Dorn is earth. Mairi is sea. And you, Dark Peace, are the sky."

"Astute of you."

"But no one to represent fire."

"We use it as we need to, as you can see." She pointed to the smoldering cauldron and the brick fire and its column of black smoke, which was thicker and more violent since Petr and Gavina had arrived.

"I see that you use it," said Gavina, "but you don't really understand it." With the white pen, she drew another symbol on the lantern, a single spiral. She chanted quiet words as she drew it. She set the lantern down and lit it, and like before, its light bloomed and pushed away the dark fog and gloom.

"The simple spiral," she said, "symbol of ethereal energy. The symbol of the flame. The fourth element, the one that is mine."

Fia eyed Dorn, who was now lying bleary-eyed on the stones, panting. She shook her head, then stepped toward the lantern. Petr moved to block her.

"Let her come, Petr. We can't guard the light every hour of every day."

He allowed Fia room to pass. She walked to the lantern and reached to pick it up. As her hand closed, white light flared from the glass and she jerked her hand back. She swore. She curled her hands into fists and let them burst open, and a great breeze rose and swirled about the lantern, catching and casting leaves and dirt and dark smoke from the cauldron. The wind rattled the lantern, pushed it so that it leaned as if about to topple. But the flame swelled like when one blows on a campfire, and the lantern remained upright. The gloom and smoke retreated further. The black column of smoke seemed to bend away.

Fia swore again. She waved her sister forward. "Mairi, quench the damn thing."

The younger sister, kicking her black shoes and looking unconcerned, jumped down from the wall. She placed her fingers on her lips, then opened her hands and chanted inaudible words. Immediately, rain fell on the castle, as if an umbrella that had been protecting them had been stolen away. Gavina and Petr tightened their cloaks, but the cold water struck their faces and ran down their necks into their inner clothing. Driving, the rain struck the lantern with a great hissing and billowing of steam, and the lantern rattled on the stone like a carnival popcorn popper sounding off, spinning in a tight circle.

The flame dimmed, but only for an instant before it found its shape and grew brighter again, punishing the offending wind and rain for challenging it. The gloom and smoke and darkness retreated further from the landing, as if a great white moon were hanging above and painting it in pale white light. Mairi stood with her unusually long arms hanging at her sides, like one wilted and washed in the rain, which had not touched her.

Dorn had recovered at this point and rushed the lantern, but the ground under his feet rumbled and buckled, and he fell to his hands and knees several feet away. He cursed and thrust his scraped, bleeding hands into his armpits.

Gavina, the white hawk... no, really a white dove, but also the Lantern Girl, just like her spiritual mother before her, the shining Aileen, lifted the still-burning lantern by the thin metal ring attached to its top and hung it on a hook in the courtyard's wall that seemed to have been placed there for just that purpose.

The rain had quenched the cauldron, and the smoke from it was white and weak; as Gavina watched, it fell to nothing. The black column of smoke from the pit fire was now just a wisp, lolling and squirming like a thin black snake writhing in the refreshing breeze that had risen from the east.

"Hmmph," said Fia. She'd walked over to lean over the castle wall overlooking the city, and the revelry growing louder. "A fair spell. But too late. The veil has been lifted, and the spirit world has entered Edinburgh." She crooked a black-nailed finger downward.

Gavina and Petr rushed to the wall. Below, the Halloween revelers were still milling about, moving between shops and taverns, which were all open and lighted. The noise of shouts and firecrackers and songs swelled as a fire may when blown. From several places, the sound of things breaking came, glass shattered as if dropped, hard blows against wood, car-horns honking. As they watched, a group of dark-clad youths blocked a car, waving their arms.

It all seemed mostly harmless pranks. But some of those who moved in the crowd carried with them odd shadows, like barely visible shrouds. The others around them paid them no more heed than they did the others. But these shadowed ones moved with purpose, and where they went, the pranks grew louder, more insistent. One such figure led a group of youths to throw rocks at a shop window, breaking the plate glass, then moving away in wicked laughter.

"Dark spirits," muttered Petr. "They lead only mischief now, but worse will come. I should know."

Fia said, "The weak minded are easily led to evil. When the spirits walk free, the people will know that evil exists in their pretty little world, and they will need us, need those they've forsaken and oppressed, to help them. And our power will rise."

Gavina ran and seized her lantern from the hook. It glowed strongly, none the worse for its trial. But she was feeling tired suddenly, as if she were the fuel keeping the flame aglow.

"Come, Petr. We must go to the streets and try to drive the spirits back to their home."

Fia chuckled. "Good luck, little hawk. You can drive some away, surely, but you can't be everywhere at once. And the spirits now walk throughout Edinburgh. And as you can see, even in the places beyond." She waved her arm to indicate the lands around the city, the hills across the water.

Petr and Gavina ran from the high courtyard, down the winding streets of the castle, through the gates and over the sloping esplanade, where a marching band was playing and costumed revelers danced. Among them were shadow people, whose looks were more real and not disguise; tall men in soldiers' uniforms, real weapons at their sides, thin-armed women with pale skin like Gavina's, whose expressions were centuries older than their skin; pale children stealing candy and garments and then running into the crowd, their eerie shadows passing with them like thin cloth caught in the breeze of their passing.

Everywhere Gavina went, the light from her lantern drove the spirits away. They shrank back into the real shadows of doorways, shops, and alleys, disappearing in the liquid darkness. But Gavina's legs had used their last strength running from the castle, and every step was like wading through dark mud. When they reached the crowd on Market Street, she moved to the entrance of one empty, dark shop to catch her breath. Petr joined her, eyeing the crowd with suspicion. The shadows of spirits moved within, a frightening number of them from where she stood.

"She's right, Petr." She paused to breathe. "I can't walk all of Edinburgh's streets with my lantern. I can't be everywhere at once, and the spirits will merely slip away and cause chaos elsewhere."

Her knees grew weak, and her head swam. Seeing her distress, Petr helped her reach a window stoop where she could rest.

"If only there were more of you," he said.

"One of Aileen was always enough." Around them the young people moved in singing and laughing groups, dressed in every manner of disguise, from zombie and sexy vampirellas, to toothy monsters and killer clowns. And among them, only recognized by Petr and Gavina, real evil spirits moved and cajoled and led the celebrants into more and more destructive pranks. The sounds of screams and things breaking and evil laughter were a grim counterpoint to the music coming from all directions.

"If only I could recruit help," she said. Around her many of the partiers were carrying lights of their own, small flashlights, cell phones with bright screens, and a few the colored wands that glowed with chemical fluorescence when the internal sections were broken and joined. She and Petr offered glow-sticks in her shop, always a big seller during nighttime outdoor events.

She couldn't be everywhere at once, but perhaps her fire could. The light from the sticks did nothing to drive away the shadow spirits, but what if that fire were hers?

"Petr, run to that shop and buy as many of the glow sticks as you can carry."

He looked puzzled. "Glow sticks?"

"Yes. Quickly, please, while I summon my strength."

Without hesitating, he left her and ran to the shop she'd pointed to, a book store and emporium that, like many of the others on Market Street, carried seasonal holiday items, including Halloween accessories. She sat and focused, drawing energy from around her, the frenetic movements of the people, the shaking of the earth beneath them, the wind blowing over her.

She heard a raven's call and looked toward its source, the castle wall, high up. There, the three young witches she'd fought stood, looking down at her. They lifted their hands and the wind rose and hard ice pellets began to fall. The ground beneath her vibrated. The partiers in the street around her took this all in-stride. It was October in Edinburgh, for god's sake, and the weather would do as it was wont.

Petr returned with dozens of pale white glow sticks in his arms, each about a foot and a half long. Between puffing breaths, he said, "I bought all they had, miss. I hope this is enough for what you're thinkin'." The raven's call came again, and he looked up where the three witches were casting spells against them. He muttered a dark curse.

"Thanks, Petr. Hand them to me one after another when I'm ready."

She stood and held her lantern before her, passing her finger over the symbol she'd written there, the simple, single spiral. The element of fire, the maker for the worthy, the destroyer in the wrong hands. But tonight, the illuminator. As she drew her finger over the symbol, the lantern flared and burned in a prism of pastel colors. People around her gasped and laughed, except for the few shadow spirits, who snarled and disappeared into the dark.

"Now, Petr. A glow stick please."

He placed one of the sticks in her outstretched hand. It felt cool and hard, lifeless like the wand of wax that it was. As some around her watched, she eased the tip of the stick into the lantern's flame. There was a flash and sizzle and the smell of burning wax, and then the stick flared at its tip. She pulled it out and it glowed at the end with a beautiful, prismatic flame. She held it high for all around her to see. Many clapped. A lone spirit looking over the crowd moaned and slipped away.

"I want one of those," said a teenage girl in a pirate costume near her, turning as if to go to a shop to buy one.

"Take this one, friend," said Gavina, handing the glowing stick to her. "Take it all over the city, and light the way for others. Pass the flame."

"Cool!" The girl fairly danced away, showing her prize to all those around. Other partiers pushed in to where Gavina and Petr stood. She lit one stick after another, each one glowing with a different flame, different colors. With each, Gavina asked the person given to run through the city, lighting the way for others. In minutes, she had lit all the sticks and given them away, and the circle of light they emitted seemed to grow and brighten the street. There were no shadow spirits in sight. The three figures on the castle wall stood motionless, watching.

She was exhausted, as only a flame could be. But when she and Petr walked toward their shop, others had heard of her, the woman with the little lantern. Young people came to her from all directions, asking her to light their glow sticks as she'd done for the others. She found that she could light even the sticks that had given up their chemical life, now dead rods of wax. The light she gave them was no less than the light from the sticks that were new.

The night passed, and despite her fatigue, her death on her own feet, she and Petr walked the town. They had to make the light grow to take the whole city, and the lands beyond. And they needed to stay awake and light the way until morning came, when the veil between the worlds would close, and the spirits be back in their world.

Days passed, and Gavina spent an afternoon doing something she had grown to love, walking all the streets of Edinburgh in the winter snow. But it wasn't a dark snow. The overcast sky was lit from above by the moon and the stars and heavenly bodies she couldn't name. The threatening sky on Samhain had been written off by the media as the result of an unexpected bomb cyclone off the coast and wildfires on the continent, even though the meteorological scientists proclaimed neither of those causes credible. In the beautiful, ethereal lightness of being that followed, no one cared.

She chose this day to walk the length of the Princes Street Gardens, admiring the rounded shapes of powdery snow over the hedges and brambles and trees of all sizes and shapes, like phantom ghouls caught out in the open on All Hallows' Ev'n and frozen there, trapped until the thawing of the spring equinox, the Wiccan Eostar. From there, she circled the castle from low down and found the magical place where she caught a glimpse of her little lantern hanging from the wall, hidden in plain sight, unbothered. For weeks now it had burned continuously, without oil being added, without her hand to adjust the wick, without someone to clean the glass.

She headed back east to the modern shops and businesses and the weekday afternoon bustle they raised, citizens of Edinburgh moving in concert, like a choreographed dance on the walks and in the streets. In many cities, they might grumble and hunch their shoulders in this breezy snow, but not here. There was a lightness and life to the city which the sky's gloom couldn't quench, but only fed.

As she approached the shop, a small figure dressed in drab gray clothing moved from a doorway shadow toward her. In a croaking, elderly voice, the figure said, "Might I have a word with you, young woman?"

"Yes, of course."

The figure pushed back its gray hood to reveal the face of a young woman.

"Fia," said Gavina.

"That was an impressive spell," said the young witch, in her normal voice, youthful, with a bit of sneer, but also a note of respect. "We won't be victim to that one again."

"It doesn't have to be a new war, Fia. We — you, me, your sister and brother — are all not very different. The past murders of witches hurt us as if we were the ones lost on the pyres. But I will never let the world burn or hide in darkness because of that shame and guilt. And you don't have to follow that path either."

Fia shook her head. "So poetic and uplifting. And naïve. We've tried the way of acceptance and outreach for hundreds of years, and the result is always the same. Promises made, but in the end, there is only persecution. My mother and the others like her have long since tired of the dream of acceptance."

"I can't deny the tragic history for our kind. But I can't give up hope. But you and I need each other, like the two curves of the Gaelic yin and yang, the symbols of balance and complimentary strength. We are two poles of the spiritual magnet, just as your mother Griselda and my ward Aileen were. Without each other to balance our ways and power, we can be nothing but a danger to our own people to those who don't follow the craft. Don't you see that?"

"I see only a fool who thinks things will ever change by doing the same thing."

"This isn't 1597," said Gavina, "the time of the great witch hunt. Nor is it the Satanic Panic. We have new ways to communicate now. Many witches are reaching out on social media. Many are joining us. We no longer have to hide in the shadows."

"Oh, that sounds dandy. It really does. But look more deeply into the media traffic and you'll find the new panic, fool. They're called conspiracy theories, and the ones spreading them don't need churches or traveling evangelists or television. They have QAnon and other haters doing it for them. You feel safe and cozy here in Edinburgh, but they'll be coming for you, for your little cute occult shop. The true evil ones will never give up their persecution."

Gavina reached in her pocket and found a business card. On the front was the name and address of her shop, Miss Aileen's Mysteries and Potions. On the back was the symbol of the simple spiral. She offered it to Fia, who took it with suspicion.

Gavina said, "Each alone, we are only one way. Together, we can change things.

You three are the ground and the earth and the air of which all things are made, but I am the spark which can give it all life. Together we can do anything."

Fia held the card up, and it disappeared in a puff of smoke.

"If I need you, I know where to find you."

Fia pulled her hood back over her head, once again a non-descript elder doddering through the streets of Edinburgh. She soon disappeared into the darkness of an alley.

When light and darkness converge, the consequence can be anything.

Back to High Street and to the shop and in the door, shaking her cloak and knocking her boots together, donning the leather slippers she kept in the alcove at the door. Petr was there, dusting potion bottles and spell books.

Gavina said, "Have you noticed? Such a lovely afternoon." She cleared papers from her desk and moved a ledger Petr had apparently laid there, open to yesterday's accounts.

Was she a fool as Fia said, to only feel the light, ignoring the dark which gave the light its purpose?

She really did need Fia, the dark one and her siblings.

"Petr, it's only three weeks until the yule. Before it comes, there are quite a few things we must do."

See C.J. Erick's story "When Darkness Falls on Edinburgh" online at Metaphorosis.
If you liked it, leave a comment. Authors love that!
Remember to subscribe to our e-mail updates so you'll know when new stories are posted.

About the story

This story was inspired by a brewing cauldron of ideas and events. I've been fascinated by witchcraft and magical realism for some time, in how they offer alternate ways to see the world, and in fact true alternate realities. Beliefs in the occult or magical in any form are the reality for the believer.

The varying and personal nature of witchcraft intrigues me. There are no formal hierarchies or governing bodies for the Craft, as it's sometimes called, so personal experience and creativity are important in one's own journey. Stones, herbs, and talismans are sensually appealing, pricking all the senses. And as a lover of all cards and card games, I was drawn to tarot — I own four decks now and several references — studying the origins of the practice and the arcana, or archetypes of the cards.

I've spent time in Salem, Mass several times visiting a son, obviously the site of the most famous witch burning in US history, and later enjoyed a trip to Edinburgh, a beautiful city in a beautiful county and nation for inspiring story ideas. Edinburgh's history of witch hunts in the Sixteenth Century and beyond are a grim reminder of the depth of human hatred and brutality, and a warning that we "modern" humans are not above similar injustice. That these "hunts" were often used as a vehicle to oppress women, and especially poor women, makes them doubly sinister.

A question for the author

Q: What's your favorite *non*-SFF book?

A: "Favorites" are always an evolving concept, based on stages of life and experience. But I'll give it a go.

Non-fiction first: *The Complete Idiot's Guide to Music Composition*, because I like to spread my modest creative talent as thinly as possible.

Fiction: The novel that sticks with me although I read it several decades ago is *The Reivers*, by Faulkner. An accessible tale by one of the country's most complex writers, and master of dense multi-page, stream-of-consciousness prose.

Honorable Mentions: *Interpreter of Maladies* by Jhumpa Lahiri, *The Lone Ranger and Tonto Fight in*

Heaven by Sherman Alexie, *A Good Scent from a Strange Mountain* by Robert Olen Butler.

About the author

CJ Erick writes in multiple genres, publishes novels in a space fantasy series, and dabbles in poetry. He lives in the Dallas area with his wife and their rescue superhero dog Saber-Girl, calls his sourdough bread starter "Ursula" (K. Le Guin), and cooks crazy-good Cajun food for a Midwest Yankee.

www.cjerickfiction.com,   facebook.com/cj.erick.9, Instagram: cee_jay_erick

Useful and Beautiful Things

E. Saxey

This suburb has rows and rows of identical 19th century houses, but when any single home is opened, it can contain wonders.

It's late in the hot afternoon when I report to the address the Guvnor sent me. A mahogany behemoth is escaping through the ground floor sash window: a George III wardrobe with claw feet. A remarkable piece of furniture, requiring a gang of four sweaty men to wrestle it through the window.

"Frankie!" I recognise one of the men as the Guvnor, the gang's coordinator. He's hauling at a claw foot, struggling with the weight. "Give us a hand, girl?" I step in and take some of his burden, protecting the wardrobe from damage as we bring it down to the ground. The men are thankful, if confused. I'm stronger than I look. The Guvnor slaps me on the back. "Ta, Frankie. This is a hell of a house. There's so much bloody junk, we've only got half of it out."

I follow him up the garden path. The back of his T-shirt reads 'St Lucian 'till I die', providing his own provenance. Alongside the path, I see marvels: a Chinese *famille-verte* floor vase, which shouldn't be standing up on the uneven lawn like that. I lay it gently on the grass. Sheltering under the hedge is a herd of six dining chairs, Queen Anne style, two of them stacked awkwardly, like animals mating.

"Sorry about your Ma, Frankie," calls the Guvnor. "You doing alright?"

I catch his anxiety and reassure us both: "I can work solo."

The Guvnor beckons me indoors, and upstairs to a sunlit study. "This place is a total hodgepodge, Frankie." He flaps his hand at walls, which are lined with shelves. Most are packed with books, but one shelf holds statuettes of gods, a dozen of them, an international pantheon. "It's a bad scene."

I wonder why he sounds dejected. There's death, here, certainly, I know the signs. This house was a man's home, he was the gravity which kept these objects together. Without him, they spin off and spill into the garden, and get damp and chipped. But estate sales are bread and butter to the Guvnor; he's a genius at house clearance, he can strip a place in a day. He helps to mitigate the tragedy of death by finding every item a new home.

"What have you found?" I ask him.

"We put it over the back, there. For safety."

Pushed to one corner of the study is a small low table. My discernment stirs: the table is circular and wooden, satinwood, 19th century—yes, 1860s—with a *pietra dura* marble chess board in the centre. My skills still function, thank goodness. Despite the worries of the last few months, I can do my job.

A chess set made of stone is laid out, ready to play.

I stop dead in the middle of the room. I can't intuit anything about the chess set.

I recognise the shape of the pieces—the nobs and planes of the ultra-traditional

Staunton design—but little else. I suppose the translucent pieces could be rock crystal from South Asia. Too vague, much too vague! I try to keep my heart from tick-tick-ticking in panic. The set is slightly uneven, the pieces not symmetrical. Handmade, perhaps by an amateur; such objects are always hard to identify. The dark pieces are carved from malachite, dark green with vivid spots like moss or mould.

"What's wrong with it?" I ask.

"Three of my boys couldn't put this bloody thing away," the Guvnor informs me. "I'll show you what it does." He plucks the dark green queen from the table, blinks, puts her back, nods. "Here, I'll show you." Picks up the queen again and replaces her. He remembers nothing, resetting before my eyes. "Wait a mo, I'll show—"

"You showed me."

"Damn! Did it mess me around, again? Well, you get the idea."

"What do the other pieces do?"

"Not a clue. But one lad who touched them was acting so funny, I had to send him home. It's all yours, if you want it. Usual terms? You take it away, fifty-fifty if you sell it on?"

That's fair, so we shake on it. The Guvnor leaves me to my work. I slough off my backpack, tie back my hair. I don't go back to the chess set, at first, but poke through the bookshelves in case there's a box for the set, or any provenance or context.

"Hey! You can't take any of those."

I jump back. I overlooked the person frowning at me from the far corner of the study, because she wasn't part of my jurisdiction. I take her in: rounded, wearing dusty dungarees, about three decades old, but people are hard to date. Her dark brown hair, in a shaggy bob, is a couple of inches longer than when we last met, and her expression is more combative.

"My employer has an agreement for the books," she says. "I work for Sotherans. I'm Tamsin Zhang."

"I know. I mean, we both worked on the Griffiths estate, in Portslade. I'm Frankie Cornish."

"That was woman with you, an older woman. She got the *Mabinogion*."

"My colleague." My mother. Yes, she took the *Mabinogion*, an 1880 edition, lavishly illustrated, cloth-covered in green. What a memory for an object Ms Zhang has. I recognise a kindred spirit. I need to reassure her. "I'm only taking the chess set."

She walks closer. Her spectacles are round, with faux tortoiseshell and strong lenses, and I think I come into focus for her because her frown relaxes.

"Oh, yes! I remember you. Why are you in my books, then?"

"Looking for anything related."

"The dead guy had a secretary, who took all his papers."

I sigh at the news. She could go back to her work, but she lingers, perhaps regretting her initial hostility. "What's so important about the chess set?" she asks, peering down at the pieces. She is 5'3", not as high as my chin. "They carried it in here like it might explode."

"I'm disposing of it."

"You're throwing it out? Can I have it?"

"No! Sorry. I mean, I'm taking it away with me. To evaluate."

"Are you taking any of this other stuff? This house is ridiculous. What was he doing with all these?" She points at the shelf of gods, where a fist-sized blue baboon (sixth century BC) hides in his newspaper wrapping from a bronze leopard (17th century, probably stolen in the sack of Benin City). Some of the gods are genuine and some are replicas, and nobody will want the whole mismatched collection, but the Guvnor will find each god a new owner.

In the second during which the gods distract me, Tamsin reaches for a chess piece.

"Don't!"

"I can be careful. I handle fragile books, that's my job." Tamsin is so sure of herself, so indignant, that I pause. She plucks up the green queen, places her down again, blinks and resets. "I'll be careful." She picks the queen up again, puts it down. The possibility of danger overrides my manners, and my hand shoots out to grab her wrist, to stop her third attempt. But Tamsin is already drawing back, and my hand closes on empty air. "Ooh, that's weird. That's *clever...*" She touches the head of the green queen, blinks a few times and laughs in astonishment. "Bloody hell."

"You have to stop. It might not be safe." I sound priggish. She doesn't seem to take offence, but does give me a hard stare, eyes huge through her distorting spectacles.

"Did you know it would do that?"

There's no chance of bluffing, she's felt the weird effect herself. "I knew it would do *something*. That's why the Guvnor called me in."

"Does this kind of thing happen often?"

"To me, yes." She looks at me with avid interest.

"So how does it work?"

"I don't know." I have a handful of hypotheses. "I have to take it away and test it."

Her frown returns, similar to when she mentioned the *Mabinogion*: unwilling to let go. "Wait! I have something that might be connected. We can investigate!"

I am so used to working with my mother that the offer of collaboration is a comfort.

The owner's name is Magnus Owens. Earlier that day, Tamsin found his diaries, which were shelved with his books and thus escaped the notice of his secretary.

"Check these out," Tamsin says. They're half-bound in Moroccan with blind tooling. "Bit creepy, other people's diaries. Not my area."

She passes me a volume. Diaries are the most personal, the least transferrable objects. I know these ones may not find a buyer, despite their fine bindings. "Are there family members who might be interested?"

Tamsin shrugs, indifferent. "Dunno. Owens doesn't mention having a wife or kids, in the parts I read. He was mining graphite in Sri Lanka, obsessed with his collections. He lists all the things he buys, there are cross-references to a stack of auction catalogues, I showed them to the Guvnor." I'm glad. That will help him re-home the objects. "But look at this." Tamsin stands close to me, turns the pages of the volume I hold, and points to the notes and number at the foot of each page: *Won in 22, Sicilian Defence, Smith-Morra Gambit. Lost in 10, Dutch Defence.* "This is the main thing, apart from collecting, that he bothers to write down. It's a record of chess games." She flips forwards, backwards. Numbers on every page.

"He played every night?"

"Yeah, almost. So, do you think he made this freaky chess set to confuse his friends? To win more games. Maybe to win money?" I admire the leaps of her logic.

But there's no money mentioned here, only a tally. I flick the pages, find a month when things improve for Owen: *Won in 12. Won in 10.* Only a week before, I find a description of his chess set arriving from Rajasthan.

As soon as I read the place-name, I am flooded by images of Rajasthani stone-carving: Jali screens framing the sky in a lattice of stars. A provenance! I feel it like a delicious cool wave. My heart calms. And the diaries have proved useful, after all.

Tamsin quizzes me, as I take photos of the relevant diary pages.

"So do you ever get called in to deal with books? Books which do weird things?"

"Sometimes."

"Magic books?"

"Not magic."

"Alright, *freaky* books. Do you have any? Could I see them?"

"Thank you, but I'm not planning to sell any. You're with Sotherans? I'll think of them, the next time I have one." She looks a little annoyed. I suppose it would have been a professional coup, for her to bring in an unusual tome. I pick up the green queen and stow her in my backpack.

"Hey. Frankie!" She touches my arm, suddenly agitated. "How can you touch the pieces, like that?"

I've made a foolish mistake. Normally I'd wear gloves, to keep up appearances. "I have a high tolerance."

"For freaky stuff." Tamsin's eyes shine. "It doesn't do anything to you?"

"I'm not very sensitive." The room is too hot. If I were staying, I'd throw up the sash windows, invite a breeze in to ruffle the packing paper. But I'm leaving.

Tamsin asks: "If you're not *sensitive*, how will you find out if the other pieces do the same thing?"

She notices too much, and she thinks too fast. I look at the ranks of chess nobility, slightly askew as if drunk, gazing over their pawn army. Each piece could be hazardous. Normally, my mother would test the pieces, at her workbench back home, with great interest and care.

"I'll help you," Tamsin offers.

"You can't."

"I can. They won't do me any real harm, will they?"

"One of the Guvnor's boys went home, sick."

"He might have skived off to enjoy the weather. I'll help you find out."

I have a book of contacts, from my mother, listing trustworthy people who buy strange things. I have storage facilities, and a network of folk (including the Guvnor) who put interesting artefacts my way. What I don't have is someone to do what my mother did: interact with objects, and let them work on her, demonstrating their properties. The nervous ticking fills my chest again.

"I won't *steal* them," she protests. "I'm a *book* person!" I think she's teasing me. I find her hard to read.

"Maybe, thank you. Yes." I make one stipulation for safety: "But not until the house is empty."

For the next few hours, Tamsin works at the far end of the study, chatting with me between periods of intense concentration. She asks me again about unusual books, and I describe a handful that I've seen, and their hazards. I tell her in the hopes she will respect my expertise, as I respect hers, but she seems unsatisfied.

At six in the evening, the shouts and crashes downstairs die away. The Guvnor hands me the keys, and the house is silent.

"So I pick the pieces up," asks Tamsin, "One at a time?"

I hold my notebook and pencil ready. "And tell me the effect."

"Just the greens, or do you think the whites do anything?"

I try to think like Magnus Owens. "He wouldn't want to disadvantage himself."

"Yeah, but could the white pieces do *positive* things?" She puts herself in the shoes of the dead man, so easily.

"Perhaps. Let's try them first." I sit on the floorboards, cross-legged by the chess table. In my experience, it's better not to have too far to fall. Tamsin sits down, not across the board where an opponent would be, but on the adjoining edge to me, our knees almost touching.

I can see how deftly Tamsin must handle delicate books. She walks her index fingers with care along the heads of the pawns. King's pawn: "Nothing." Knight's pawn: "Nothing." I write, for both: *No effect.*

Bishop's pawn: Tamsin sneezes violently. Her bobbed hair falls forwards.

"It wasn't the pawn! It's dust." *No effect/allergenic?*

Rook's pawn: "I feel calm. Really chill." *Relaxing?* Then she looks about the room and sighs. From up on the shelf of gods, the small blue baboon watches us. "This damn house. Why don't I have a house like this, a collection like this? Oh, hang on." She throws the pawn from hand to hand. "It's this piece. It makes me feel like I deserve everything."

"Confidence?"

"Entitlement. Resentment."

Queen's pawn: "Oooh. This one feels *nice*." Tamsin clutches it to her chest. "Satisfying. Like dumplings. Maybe I'm just hungry." She lifts her arms over her head, savouring the stretch, and regards me with a catlike smile. *Sense of wellbeing?* "What do you want?"

"Sorry?"

She's taken out her phone. "Wonton soup?"

"Dim sum," I say, for the sake of appearances.

"It'll be here in half an hour, you owe me a tenner." Her fingers take three last steps along the front rank of pieces: rook's pawn, bishop's pawn, knight's pawn. "And these are all duds. You could let me have one as a souvenir."

"I have to keep the set together." But perhaps I should pay her half of what I make from the set, because her evaluation will inform me about how to sell it. Not on the open market, of course, but using my mother's list of trustworthy collectors. I would have to stay in contact with Tamsin, to arrange payment. The prospect cheers me.

Tamsin plucks up the white bishop and squints at a bookcase, more than three metres away. "I can read all the titles." She takes off her glasses. "Hey, my eyesight's fine. Holy crap! Has this thing fixed my eyes?"

"It may have optimised how your brain works with your eyes." *Positive minor visual effects*, I write.

"Wow. Can I buy it, seriously?" Her glasses have left a pink dent on each side of her nose. "My eyes are so rubbish, this would be a life-changer."

"We don't know how it works. It could be doing terrible damage to your brain."

White bishop is grudgingly replaced, as are Tamsin's glasses, and she scoops up the white knight. "I feel confident." She chuckles. "No, I feel *lucky*."

"Shall we test it?" In my pocket, I find two dice and hand them over.

Her expression is sceptical, but she sends the dice rattling across the floorboards. Two sixes. I retrieve them, and Tamsin rolls them again. Double sixes. I write *positive effect, good fortune* while she glares at the white bishop, its eyeless face and aghast mouth.

"So this little blobby boy is actually affecting the world," says Tamsin. "But double sixes are a completely arbitrary symbol. How does it know that they're lucky? Wait, are those dice loaded?"

"I can give you a coin to toss, if you'd rather."

She stands and paces back over to the bookshelves. Impossible questions are grinding together in her mind. She's probably going to leave, now. I may not see her again, except at contentious estate sales, at intervals of years. That's alright. People are allowed to relocate themselves.

Tamsin uses both hands to unshelve a large dictionary, Bosworth and Toller's Old English, cloth-bound in burgundy, and carries it back to me. She opens the cover carefully. Inside, the pages have been hollowed out to hide a flat bottle of Talisker 25 year single malt whisky. "I found it this morning. Isn't it tacky?" She upends the bottle into her mouth and there's an audible glug. She hands it over to me.

"I don't know if we should combine alcohol with…"

"We totally should, because people are going to play with these pieces when they're drinking sherry, or what-have-you, and you need to know how bad that would be." She folds her legs up and re-joins me on the floor. She's misjudged our proximity, and now her knee presses mine. "I bet Owens got his friends drunk, the filthy cheat. Why do you have dice in your pocket? Does this kind of thing happen to you a lot, eh?"

"I have some cufflinks which work the other way. Gold with blue enamel." Translucent lapis blue over hatched engine-turning. They're in my mother's permanent collection, never to be sold. "Fabergé."

"Unlucky cufflinks?"

"Three owners found them… difficult." I realise I'm showing off. I shouldn't. It's dangerous to invite her to look closely at my life.

"Wow. *Terminally* difficult? And you kept them? William Morris wouldn't like that." She prods my shoulder and takes back the whisky bottle from my hands. I want to share her joke but I can only think of William Morris' floral patterns, looping across mid-C19th sofas.

"Why would he care about my cufflinks?"

"He said you shouldn't have anything in your house that you don't know to be useful, or believe to be beautiful. But your house is full of *awful* stuff, by the sound of it. Am I right?"

I think of my mother's workbench, and all the artefacts my mother restored and rehomed. Then the wall of strongboxes, one of which will hold the chess set. I picture the peace that will fill me when I close the lid. "It's a very useful place, overall."

"Oh, Frankie, you should have a beautiful house!" This time it sounds less like a scolding than a wish: Tamsin thinks I deserve a beautiful house. Before I can ask her, she adds: "What's your favourite thing that you own? Is it a book?"

I've never thought of that. I don't truly consider the objects in my collection to be mine. They're only resting with me because nobody else can own them, at present. "I don't have a favourite."

"Not even that *Mabinogion* you snatched?" Another nudge on my shoulder. "Was it freaky? What did it do?" It could be a joke, but perhaps her excellent memory for books is supported by a great capacity for grudges. I shake my head.

White rook: "Nothing. No, wait." She holds out her wrist. Should I admire her bracelet of 1970s cloisonné beads, patterned with bats? "My pulse. Feel it."

I touch her warm soft wrist, and the flicker I find there slows and slows. "You should put the rook down."

"But I feel really calm. Really on top of things..." I pluck the rook from her hand. *Induces catatonia?* "Spoil-sport," she accuses, rubbing her wrist where I touched it. "The queen's got to be the most powerful one, right?" She lowers her fingertip onto the milky crown of the white queen. "Oh. I'm the most important person in the world. Anything I do for my own benefit is just fine. Cool." *Solipsism?*

White king: "Wow. The board just lit up." Tamsin sits bolt upright. "I can see all the moves. I haven't played chess since I was ten, but I can see every way it could possibly go..."

She turns her gaze on me, and lapses into silence.

I write down *strategic foresight.*

"How do you get into a job like yours?" she asks, still staring.

I write *overly curious,* because I know she's reading it.

"No, but seriously. It can't just be because you're *insensitive.*"

Persistent intrusive questioning. I shouldn't have shown off about my cufflinks. I need to turn her attention aside. "Is there more whisky?"

Tamsin reluctantly relinquishes the white king. "I can't keep it?"

"It might give you something like concussion."

"But you're still going to sell the set?"

The list of people I would trust with them has dwindled with each piece, each power. "I'll see."

"Or get rid of them. Throw them away."

"No! Don't say that!"

"Why not? God, you sound like those people who get sentimental over books being chucked out. Do you know how many terrible, waste-of-space books there are? You can't hang on to *everything,* you can just bung stuff in the bin..."

I shake my head, over and over. I worry I might scream.

A chime rings round the room. Tamsin springs to her feet. "Food's here!"

Tamsin thunders down the stairs, and the vibrations set one of the shelf-gods wobbling. I nudge it further back, to safety. I would love to have a day to hold each of the small statues in my hands and know who they are, where they come from. But they're not dangerous, so they're not my business.

I should be wary of Tamsin. She lulled me into thinking of her as my work partner, but I didn't choose her. She keeps teasing me and touching me, but I should keep a level head. I hear her chatting with the delivery man, which gives me time to pluck up all the pieces we've tested and stash them in my bag, away from temptation.

When Tamsin returns, her face is somewhat pallid. "The delivery guy told me that Owens *died* here. In the house."

I remember the Guvnor saying this was a *bad scene*, and wonder if he meant the manner of Owen's death. "It's understandable." People die. Things endure.

"It's grim." Tamsin lays the pots of food out on the floor. "Hey, where did the white pieces go?"

"They're safe. What do you think Owens was like?" I ask, to distract her from my tidying, and from the fact that I won't eat the dim sum. And because I want to know her opinion.

"An English man collecting colonial curiosities to make his Englishness more interesting." She puts herself in Owen's place, then puts him in his place, too.

"Did you get that from his diaries?"

"I got that from his book collection—lots of international publications, lots of uncracked spines. Don't be sad! All the better for my bosses, to have pristine Bengali poetry. *Gitanjali* will end up with someone who appreciates it."

I wait until Tamsin wrangles a steamed dumpling into her mouth. "The green pieces," I say. "I shouldn't let you test them."

"*Let* me, hah." She can still argue with her mouth full.

"The green ones may be terrible."

"No, because look..." She swigs her coke. I've hidden the whisky under my backpack. "They can't be that godawful, or nobody would ever play chess with him twice. They're not going to make you cough up your lungs, are they?" She's three moves ahead of me. "And *you* need to know how they work. Don't you? To be a good caretaker."

I need to know the full extent, to judge what to do with the set: who might safely buy it, or more likely, how I can store it. Whether to seal it in clay or submerge it in running water. But must I rely on Tamsin?

"Let's just do the pawns," she offers, as a compromise. "They're only small."

The pawns will perplex us both.

King's pawn: "Nothing." No effect. "It's not doing anything at all." She chuckles slyly.

"Tamsin, are you lying?"

"Nooo, heh-heh." I write *Induces duplicity/hysteria?* Tamsin shivers. "Holy hell, that was stranger than the eyesight thing."

"And it made you lie?"

"It didn't do anything! I was fine. Heh-heh."

I reach to take back the pawn, and she makes a fist, twists and turns, play-wrestles my fingers with her own. I don't like to look strong, and she's wily and enjoying herself, so the fight goes on for longer than it needs to. When the pawn is out of her hand, she asks: "Why would that help Owens win? I suppose it would encourage his opponent to cheat."

Bishop's pawn: Tamsin sighs. "I'm rubbish at this, anyway."

"At chess?"

"At everything." *Hopelessness.*

Knight's pawn: "I want to bet you a lot of money that I'm going to win." *Risk seeking? Over-confidence?* "What happens if—" Before I can stop her, she's palmed two pawns simultaneously. "Ha! I think I'm going to lose and I don't care, I still want to bet on it! I wish you could feel this!" Her grin is contagious, her eyes are alight. This is all irresponsible, reprehensible. I should be working alone.

"Stop. Please." Thankfully, she does.

Queen's pawn: "It's telling me just do anything, move wherever, don't overthink it."

Hazardous rashness. "Does it have a voice?"

"No, it's just a feeling. Do some things have voices?"

I think of the rooms in my mother's house—my house—filled with items that charmed and berated her, to which I am blessedly oblivious. We were perfect colleagues. "Sometimes."

She leans in closer to me. Does she want to be hugged? I could do that. She swipes the whisky from under my bag. "Queen's pawn makes you thirsty."

Rook's pawn makes Tamsin jump to her feet, knocking over the remnants of her takeaway. "Sorry! I can't sit still." *Restless.* "Why does he get all this stuff? How can anyone deserve..." *Psychologically restless?* "I feel small. Do I seem small?"

"Not more than you—no."

"You're not taking me seriously!"

I should have said something kinder, more respectful. "I'm sorry. Put the pawn down?"

Instead, she sweeps up more pieces, handfuls of them, stuffing them into the pockets of her dungarees, and runs.

I lunge at her but she's quicker. She's off down the stairs, almost flying, bursting out of the back door and vanishing into the overgrown garden.

I have to follow. It's dusk, and the trees cast deep shadows. There's a pale path, but as I run down it, chasing her, I feel thorns catch at my clothes. I hear Tamsin, rather than see her, ahead of me. Please let her not be hurt. Let her not drop anything, either. Let me not have to hunt for the dark green chess pieces amid brambles in the dark.

My eyes adjust and a movement draws my gaze to Tamsin standing in an old wooden gazebo. I should jump at her, pin her arms, make her release the rook's pawn. But I can't imagine hurting her.

"Come on! Take them off me." She raises her fist and waves it from side to side. "This is most the important thing, right?"

It is an accusation, but it is true. People pass, things endure; my responsibility is to things. While I hesitate, I see a quick arc in the dark, her arm as she flings the pawn of low self-esteem far into the garden.

Her penitence is instant. "Oh, God, sorry! Shit! I'll find it!" Her face glows in the light of her phone. "It went in that direction..."

I have a keyring torch, and I spot the pawn before she does, resting in a patch of dandelions. I turn my back to Tamsin before I stoop to pick it up. I need to keep it secure. I dust off the dirt and place it on my tongue, force myself to swallow, feel the nobbles as it slides down my throat.

"Found it," I call.

"I've found something else." Tamsin has her phone light trained on a flickering tail of plastic tape in the bushes, with lettering: POLICE LINE DO NOT CROSS. "I think he died in the garden. Owens." Tamsin stares up at the house, the sash window glowing with light. "Maybe he jumped out of the window of his study. Do you think the chess set killed him?"

I thought not: he should have known its properties. But what pieces might he have touched by accident, in what combination? Did he grab recklessness, self-doubt, and foresight all in one hand, and throw himself away? And now all his possessions have followed him, flung outwards, dispersing.

Tamsin, standing beside me, says: "You'll get rid of it, won't you?"

"Don't worry. I won't pass it on to another owner."

"No, I mean you should trash it. Smash it up and bury it."

I dislike this line of thought. I dislike it very much. Inside me, things tick painfully fast.

The horrible plastic police tape dances about in the wind. I am seized by a pang of fear. I'm not mourning Owen, or thinking of the ways he might have died; I'm empathising with the objects he's left behind. I never want to be wrapped in a rug, left on a lawn. I don't want to be forced to seek someone new, someone who appreciates me enough to keep me.

My internal mechanisms are spinning wildly. I need to be calm. I remind myself: I may not have an owner, but I have a place in the world. I have earned it.

I duck into the gazebo and sit on the bench I find inside. "You can't throw an artefact away," I say. "Just because you don't have a use for it at the moment." I'm speaking to myself more than to Tamsin.

She hears me, though, and shouts back: "But you can't hang onto it indefinitely, either. Not if it's toxic!"

"I'll keep it safe."

"But you won't live forever, will you?"

I don't know the answer to that.

Tamsin stumbles into the gazebo and joins me on my bench, pulling out her bottle of coke (into which, it occurs to me, she has poured a lot of the whisky) and drinking deeply.

"Let's do the rest of them quickly," she offers.

I shake my head.

"But we're almost done." She points to her dungaree pocket. I see the bumps of the stolen pieces through the denim. "You get them out."

I work my hand into her pocket, ignoring the warmth of her body, and retrieve them. I line them up on the bench, within arm's reach, and lay my torch alongside, to light them. I take out my small notebook and pen. I can complete this quickly and depart.

Green rook: "I shouldn't be here," says Tamsin.

"The same as the rook's pawn?"

"No, that was just twitchy legs. This is: I need to get away, right now! Shit, do you think this is the one that killed Owens? Sit on my feet. Come on, it'll slow me down if I try to run off." She's tucking a foot under the bend of my knee, wriggling it until it's wedged. "There, like that."

Need to be elsewhere? Self-destruction? My handwriting is not neat.

Green bishop: "Do you ever wonder what you're for?"

I did. I do. Has the bishop given her telepathy? If so, does she know how conscious I am of her wriggling foot?

"Go on, write down *existential doubt.* Or *moody cow.*"

Green knight: "I want to fight you. I hate you!" She wrenches her foot free from under my leg, but falls backwards to the floor. I spring up, hit a gazebo pillar and shake down cobwebs and dust onto both of us. I want to help Tamsin stand, but her arms are flailing, she is still furious at me. She takes a wild swing. The chess piece flies from her hand. "Gah! Vicious little horse bastard!" she cries.

I crouch down to pick up the knight, and quickly swallow it, to join the pawn. I am the safest temporary store for small, wicked objects.

Before I can stand, a hot hand lands on my back. I hear Tamsin's breath. Her hand slides up, she slips her fingers into my hair, to stir deliciously against my scalp.

"You're a very attractive—whatever you are. A very cute curator."

Her voice is low and tender, all her rage boiled away, and her heat warms me. But only one of her hands is in my hair.

She's holding the green king in the other.

It's not fair to let this go on. I twist around and prise her fingers open as gently as I can.

I know it's worked when I hear her swear, and she pulls away from me and stomps to the other side of the hut.

I eat the green king. I focus on finding my notebook. I write: *Emotional connection?* A euphemism. The lust-inducing king is even less explicable than the rage-knight. Would desire distract your opponent? It's distracted Tamsin, who is holding her head in her hands.

The aphrodisiac effects of the green king have disgusted her. And I'm to blame, I wanted to impress her by my association with wonderful things. My back feels chilly, now, where her hand had rested.

Tamsin raises her head, sucks in the night air. "Is that the last one?" she asks, faintly.

"There's only one piece left, and we know what she does. The green queen."

"Oh! Her." The monarch of forgetting and re-setting. Maybe Tamsin would appreciate some amnesia.

I look back to the house, and through the back door glimpse floorboards of rich golden oak. Carpets fade and moths consume them, but wood goes on for centuries. Until you burn it. Even then, it's useful.

"You have to get rid of them all," Tamsin instructs me. "Apart from the one which fixed my eyesight..."

"White bishop."

"You could give that one to a doctor. All the others, though, they need to go! You can't let people use them to start fights, or win elections. Or as a bloody truth drug."

I can't read my notebook, so I double-check my mental list of the pieces; none of them worked as a truth drug. Her anger's making her exaggerate. "I'll keep them away from anyone," I promise her, as I pick up my backpack. "I'll use my best strong-room."

"But you could fall under a bus tomorrow. They'll get out into the world again. Why not destroy them?"

Tick-tick-tick, my heart stutters, faster than I've ever felt it. I can't speak my objection.

"They're lethal!" she insists. "They might have killed their last owner!" I know the fuel for her hate isn't the self-destructive bishop, or the aggressive knight. It's the green king, the piece that made her want me. "*And* they're ugly! They're failing the William Morris test on both fronts."

"I do believe that almost everything can find a new owner."

"Really? How long have you been hoarding those murderous cufflinks? Objects have to earn the space they take up in the world! Things have to be useful..."

And to my surprise, tears well up in my eyes and drip onto the golden oak floorboards.

"Not you! I didn't mean you! Oh, damn..." She scrambles across the bench to wrap her arms around me. "You're remarkable."

"Am I?" My mother did a lot of work to make me appear ordinary. "Is it obvious?"

Tamsin continues her clumsy hug and clumsy reassurance. "No, no, not unless you look really closely." People don't usually look at me closely. "I'd never have noticed, except the white king made me understand how things worked. Oh, and then you ate those chess pieces."

I clear my throat. "I've lost my mother." My co-worker, the one who restored me.

Almost all my memories are from after she mended me. "She died, two months ago, she died."

"I'm sorry."

"This is the first job I've been on, without her. I need to know I can still do the work, that I'm useful."

Tamsin loosens her grip and I think she'll let me go but she settles into a more sustainable embrace. "I understand. Everyone wants to be useful."

"But every thing *needs* to be useful."

Tamsin shakes her head very hard, brushing her face against mine. "No, no, no. You don't need to be useful."

"I do."

She is trying to think of arguments against all her earlier pronouncements. "Beautiful! You could be beautiful, instead."

I want to correct her: no, someone else must *believe* I'm beautiful.

I want to ask: does she believe I'm beautiful?

Instead, I ask: "Which chess piece makes you tell the truth?"

Tamsin buries her face in my shoulder without answering. It is the green king, then. I study her cloisonné bracelet in the dimness and listen to the tick-tick-ticking of my heart.

See E. Saxey's story "Useful and Beautiful Things" online at Metaphorosis.
If you liked it, leave a comment. Authors love that!
Remember to subscribe to our e-mail updates so you'll know when new stories are posted.

About the story

My most obvious inspiration was all the magical objects in fantasy fiction. Some of them are owned by a sinister religious order or kept in a secret government warehouse, where they can sit for decades. But if an object is in private hands, it would probably come back onto the market when the owner died, so how would the antiques trade handle it? I thought it would require a small team of specialists, taking the proper precautions to nullify curses or contain startling powers. The specialists would be well respected, but not showy, brought in by word-of-mouth recommendations.

What pushed the story onwards was the essential strangeness of collections, and their need for an owner to give them meaning. If I look around my study, every object makes sense to me; they're an external map of my interests and experiences, past and present. If I die, then it's just a roomful of junk. Nobody will be able to tell: did I love that book, or had I never got around to reading it? Where did that pebble come from? The key has been lost, the message is meaningless. I became fascinated by the restorative work of finding a new owner for an object, a new home, and thus a new meaning. Something as mundane and brusque as house clearance becomes a very kind, respectful process. I combined these two concerns — handling magical objects, and rehoming things as a restorative act — and together they conjured up my main character.

A question for the author

Q: What do you think is the single most important quality for a good writer to possess?

A: I think a writer's most important quality could be the capacity to stand back from the work and evaluate how it will be read by others. It's an incredibly difficult work of strategic amnesia — you know what you wanted to convey, but you have to forget that, to see whether your meaning actually comes across from what's on the page. And you also know what's going to happen next in the plot, but have to evaluate whether you've laid enough groundwork, or over-egged the pudding. Reading groups or partners are invaluable, because they're genuinely fresh eyes, although you have to get past the exchange of polite compliments and ask really big basic questions: what time period do you actually think it's set in? Did you notice that this character confessed to murder? And you can't get readers in at every sentence. So being able to do it alone is necessary, and ten times harder.

About the author

E. Saxey is a queer Londoner who works in Universities and volunteers in libraries. Their current writing desk used to belong to the Ancient Order of Druids.

thelightningbook.co.uk, @esaxey

The Beast-Consul

E.C. Dorgan

It's the best day of the year for a Consul. Five hundred guests invited to the national day reception, and most of them are here, clapping while the Consul climbs up to the stage. There's the host-country Foreign Minister, the Chief of Protocol, the Dean of the Diplomatic Corps. The Consul spies a little girl in the second row, in a grey dress. She makes a mental note to approach the girl later, and tell her she too, one day, can be Consul.

There's a hush while the audience waits. By some miracle, every cell phone is silent. The Consul touches her helmet— her hair, and pushes down her doubts.

"Esteemed guests."

A bird with black, indigo, and orange feathers flies over the stage. The Consul's voice trails while she watches it. By the time she remembers her guests, cell phones are ringing and everyone's talking. The Foreign Minister's chair is empty. Her audience lost, she starts to speak.

She sits in her office after the reception, watching birds out her window while her staff bring her papers. She writes 'approved' and signs her name without reading. Two years at post, and she still doesn't know how to be Consul. Her bunions ache and her nylons chafe. She's dying to take off her sharp heels and cracking makeup but she's wanted at a dinner. They're always the same—her diplomatic colleagues laughing and clinking glasses with their more gregarious counterparts, the Consul alone with her plate.

The other diplomats attribute her silence to some national quirk, but the Consul knows better. She's still that strange little girl from the woods north of the capital, under the cover of helmet hair and a title she'll never be fit for.

It's past dark when she returns to the Official Residence. She needs both hands to take off her heels. Her husband meets her in the kitchen, wearing fuzzy socks. He holds out a colourless rose.

"Our anniversary." He kisses the top of her head.

She tells him she needs air.

She steps outside to the garden. Her bare toes breathe in the night. The garden is the only part of her job that she likes. During the day, it's all vehicle exhaust and traffic. But after dark, it's magical. She can smell the night-blooming roses, touch their tender petals.

She feels her cheeks and finds them wet. The next instant, she's sobbing. She doesn't need to look up to know it's the moon. She cries every time it's full. Some nights, she doesn't stop until morning. The moon reminds her of her childhood, how she spent too much time alone in the woods, reading. How she lost herself there. She wishes she could remember what part of her is missing.

She tastes dread when she wakes up in the morning. Steels her toes for her pointed heels and her face for the camouflage of makeup. It's too much. She takes out her phone and searches until she finds a forest. Brings the screen to her nose so she can smell the plastic and see all the thumbprints. That night, instead of staring at the ceiling unsleeping, she watches the trees until morning.

The next thing she knows, she's skipping receptions and sending 'regrets' to dinners. Googling trees during meetings. One day, she's in a tough negotiation when she has a revelation. The thought rocks her entire being. She stops the session and rushes with her phone to the bathroom. Locks herself in a stall and zooms to make the screen big. Presses her nose into the forest, utterly certain, for once, what would fix her—to learn the secret name of trees.

All day at work, she stares into the phone. In the evening, she closes herself in her home office and watches the forest some more. Her eyes strain. She misses deadlines and neglects to eat. She forgets her son's birthday. And something stranger—she remembers things.

At first it's nothing—bright colours, indescribable smells. They come to her when she's signing documents, or watching her trees. Her husband asks if she's okay. Soon she's seeing whole scenes—forests, dragonflies, pine trees. She gets flashes while giving speeches. She has to grip the podium with both hands now. One day, she draws a dragonfly on a document. She scribbles over it, but her staff bring it back to her, seeking clarification.

She's in her office one night, toes in the rug, bunions aching, when a memory returns in a rush. When she was still that little girl in the forest, long before she was Consul, a monster and the moon came down to her. She can still see the shine of the moon, reflecting so bright it burned her eyes, and the sound—how could she forget it—of that stretching of her heart from forest to sky. The sound of it snapping like gum, the monster with its teeth dripping red.

She buys gum and puts all five pieces in her mouth at once to try to make sense of it. She chews and smacks and stretches the gum between her teeth, but all that she feels is emptiness.

One night, sitting in her office, the Consul gets a call from headquarters. It's the Head of department—the Consul's boss. She instructs the Consul to report back to the Ministry by the end of the week for 'consultations'. The Consul makes the arrangements. She knows it's a euphemism, like everything in diplomacy.

On her first day in the capital, the Consul wears a grey power suit and slips on her sharpest heels. She puts on two layers of foundation, and sprays extra hairspray on her hair. She looks in the mirror, but she doesn't see a diplomat.

She spends the day in meetings. People in ashen suits call her 'Consul' and take notes when she speaks. It's stultifying. Her nylons itch. Her mind is on the forest in her phone. She touches her helmet-hair and wonders how she became this thing.

There's the hanging threat of a working dinner, but the Consul needs to breathe. She leaves the Ministry and walks two blocks to a park. It's nothing fancy—dying grass and a pond that's more of a puddle. The Consul walks around it. The uneven pitch of the grass hurts her bunion, and her pencil skirt limits her step.

She walks in circles and loses track of time. The sun descends behind buildings, and the nearby road quiets. She looks up and sees ducks in the water. Their necks are bright green, and when they swim, their rears waggle. The Consul smiles. The next time she looks, the sky is dark and the ducks are long gone.

Her phone buzzes and when she checks it, she sees five unanswered calls. She's missed her dinner. She returns to the hotel and kicks off her shoes. It feels good to throw her nylons in the garbage, though she has another pair laid out for tomorrow. She studies her reflection. Her helmet hair's held, but her foundation is cracked and all she can see of her makeup is lipliner.

For the first night in weeks, she doesn't pull up her cellphone forest. Instead, she looks up ducks. Each search leads to another query. Two hours and many

Internet wormholes later, she finds herself making an appointment for a therapist. She has no idea how googling ducks has led her there.

The next day, she finishes her meetings early to get to her appointment. A blast of essential oils hits her when she walks into the therapist's office. The scent might be pine, but it burns her nostrils—it's nothing like the imagined perfume of her forest.

The therapist exudes confidence—she would make a good diplomat. She asks the Consul about her job. The Consul tells her she signs papers. She asks her about her marriage. The Consul says her husband remembers anniversaries. She asks about her son. The Consul describes what he's reading. The therapist asks if she's happy.

The Consul looks out the window. There's no bird outside to save her. She wants to tell the therapist she's a fake, that she doesn't know what to say at dinners, or what to do with all those papers. She wants to tell her how she doesn't love her husband, and how when she looks at her son, she doesn't know how to be a mother.

Instead, she tells the therapist the one thing she promised herself she wouldn't share. She tells the therapist how she cries under the moon, and how she lost herself so many years ago, when she was just a little girl in the forest. She tells the therapist how she knows what would make her better, how she'd throw away every diplomatic privilege and title, just to taste, for one fleeting moment, the rounded syllables of the forest's secrets.

The therapist's eyes widen. She opens her notebook and writes. At the end of their hour, she declares they'll need more sessions. The Consul says she'll check her schedule. She walks out of the therapist's office and resolves never to go back.

Back at the hotel, the Consul peels off her godawful nylons and rubs the budding bunion on her foot. If only she could throw her heels out the window...

Her phone buzzes with an incoming message. She reads it and wants to toss her phone away too. Instead, she pulls out another pair of nylons and reaches for her heels. Stares at her cramped toes in the elevator, wishing it would descend slower. When the doors open, her husband greets her. He holds out a grey rose. His face, as usual, is blank.

"Surprise dear, I'm here."

Her son steps out behind him. His face says he'd rather be reading.

They go to a restaurant. Her husband says their son spent the day choosing it. The Consul doesn't believe it. Her son's like her. Even now, lingering over his pasta, his eyes are elsewhere. Her husband's the sentimental one. The one who wants this facade of family. He reaches his hand out to touch her. She doesn't pull away. She forces a smile— that's what diplomats do.

Her eyes start to tear after dinner, when they're waiting for the bill. No need to look outside to know it's the moon rising. She excuses herself to go to the washroom. When she looks at her reflection, the tears are already streaming.

The Consul's most important meeting is the next day, with the Head of department, in her office on the executive floor. The Consul has never been up there. When she steps out of the elevator, the first thing she notices is the different carpet. It's the colour of smoke, and it cushions her toes, even her bunion. When she steps, her heels are silent.

She arrives at the Head of department's office and sees the Head of personnel is there too. It makes the Consul uneasy. The Head of department doesn't acknowledge her. She types and hits send on an email, then picks up the phone to ask about a briefing note. Her slate suit is designer and her helmet's immaculate.

The Consul looks out the window and waits. After ten minutes, the Head of department points to the mints on her desk.

"Take one."

The Consul complies.

The Head of department takes off her glasses. She finally looks at the Consul. "How are you doing, really?"

An impossibly orange bird lands on the outside ledge. The Consul's eyes follow it. The Head of personnel opens her notebook. It hurts to look away from the bird, but the Consul needs her wits. The Head of department watches her, unblinking. It occurs to the Consul that these 'consultations' have nothing to do with bilateral relations and everything to do with how she's doing 'really'.

When the Consul starts to speak, the Head of personnel picks up her pen. She writes more notes than the therapist. At least the Consul avoids mentioning trees. Precisely twelve minutes after it's started, the Head of department declares the meeting over. She picks up the phone and says she needs that briefing note. She doesn't look at the Consul.

The Consul comes away with an extra five days of leave and instructions to 'decompress'. The Head of personnel escorts the Consul out of the office. She tells the Consul she cares, but she's looking into her phone and typing a message when she says it.

Her husband finds a cabin in the woods north of the capital. The Consul can't work the kettle, and she's afraid of the propane-powered stove. But the setting's incredible. Those ducks from the city are nothing like the birds in these woods. On her first day, she sees an enormous blue bird with a magenta beard, a bright orange and black bird with a yellow stripe, and a tiny purple bird whose chirp sounds like a dragon or a train engine. And the trees—each time she looks outside, they take her breath. Her little forest on the screen pales in comparison. And their perfume, evergreen, is so much more than she ever dreamed.

Their first morning in the woods, her husband makes her breakfast in bed: homemade scones, blueberry jam, and hot coffee. By the time she gets dressed, he's back in the kitchen, making a batch of brownies. Her son is in the woods, probably reading. Growing up, she was always in the woods too, with a book. She wonders if he watches birds.

Her husband hums while he mixes batter. The Consul watches him and pours a second coffee. He's always been a different creature. Nothing like her and her son. At least he bakes. He pours the batter, and for a split second, the tune he's humming wavers, and his sleepy eyes go sharp. The Consul blinks, and he's back on-key, his eyes are once again soft. The therapist said she had imagination.

The Consul can't figure out where the days go. Her husband makes a different pastry for breakfast every morning. He bakes more brownies than they can possibly eat. In the evening, he barbecues hamburgers. One night, he gets mustard on his shirt and they laugh like a family. When the sun goes down, he makes a campfire and they roast marshmallows and listen for loons. Her son surprises her with his knowledge of them. The moon rises, but she's surrounded by trees, so she only cries a little bit.

By the fourth day of her 'decompression', the Consul's had enough of watching her husband bake. She puts on boots—so much better than heels—and pulls her hair into a ponytail. She takes a compact out of her purse and squints into the glass. It's been days since she's looked in a mirror. There's powder stuck to the glass, it makes her face soft and hazy. She looks decades younger without her helmet.

When she steps outside, the first thing she notices is how the soft earth cushions her feet, even her bunion. She breathes in spruce and pine, and regrets spending the previous days indoors.

She walks out to the trees, and takes in a world beyond that pond in the city. Her night-time garden pales. To think, she wasted all that time staring into that screen. *This* is a forest. Her fingertips brush on silken tree needles while she walks. She's never touched anything so soft. The perfume wafts up from her fingers. It makes her light-headed, almost giddy. She marvels at the clubmosses and lichens. She used to play with them when she was little, in these same woods. Dragonflies flit, bright reds and blues. She didn't know the world contained so many of them.

She stops in front of a towering pine. Can't even breathe when she looks at it. The whole universe is there in its branches. When she touches her palm to its bark, it thrums electric and vital. She closes her eyes and asks for its name. She waits, then continues walking. The forest keeps its secrets.

She only knows it's past dinner when the moon rises, glimmering behind pines, and the tears start to flow from her eyes. She should go back to the cabin. Her husband will be worried. Her son won't know she's gone. But now, reunited with dragonflies, the thought pains her. She could spend a lifetime here. There was a time she thought she would.

A memory surfaces. She was tired of being that weird child, reading books under pines, playing with clubmosses. The other girls were going places. They'd be important, Consuls maybe. She wanted to be like them.

For a while, she almost was. She made a career, she got promoted. She married her husband. She had a son. Never mind that inside she felt dead.

She stops walking. She's about to turn back, but that's when she sees it—a light, red and gleaming, behind the farthest trees.

The Consul's stepping between trees, deeper and deeper into the forest. The red beacon isn't nearing. She's on the verge of being lost. There are bears in these woods, and worse things. She almost remembers.

She's about to give up when the air changes. Her nose is stuffy from crying, but when she breathes, it's undeniable—

damp and rot, a whisper of fungus, and something else.

The scent gets stronger as she moves to the light. She trips on a log and almost tumbles. She sees it when she straightens —a clearing in the trees, a pile of logs in the centre, slick with moisture, and shining blue and orange with saprophytes. And under the logs, expanding in every direction, all the way to her own two feet, the earth is bursting with ghost pipe. It's too bright for her eyes, even under moonlight.

But it's what's sitting on the logs that takes her breath. The source of that gleam she's been tracking all night. She sucks in her breath.

The monster's ear flickers, and it starts to turn its head. Eyes fix on her, red flames. They were easier to look at through trees. Looking into them, her eyes sting. She drops her gaze as the monster pulls back its lips. Its incisors are longer than her arms.

The monster stretches its lips farther, and the Consul loses her breath. Her knees no longer support her. Behind the terror of those sharp, blood-dripping incisors, she sees what she lost all those years ago in the forest. She can barely make out the shape, but for once in her life, she's certain. There, behind fangs, is her bright red beating heart.

The memories rush back in a flood. The monster was smaller then, more of a pup than a beast, with sharp baby teeth. It's not so young now. There's grey around its muzzle, a fleck of white on its chest. Its fangs are brown and rotting.

A dragonfly lands on its snout, reflecting bright blue in the moonlight. The Consul watches it. She didn't know there were nighttime dragonflies. The monster shifts and the whole forest shudders. Her teeth rattle. She imagines her husband pausing his baking while the ground rumbles under him, and across the ocean, the petals of her nighttime roses vibrating.

When the monster focuses on her, her own heart jumps in its teeth. Her brain screams at her to run. But instead, she watches in horror, as her arm starts to extend, and her fingers reach out, grasping. The Consul wants to recoil, and to walk—no, run, back to the cabin. But her feet are stepping in the wrong direction. She's walking, arms forward, toward the monster, her body insisting on reunion with that lost piece of her.

She steps up on a log. Grabs a handhold and climbs higher. The saprophytes on the wood make her palms slip. She perseveres. Now she's only a few feet from the monster. Her whole body is trembling. The dragonfly spooks. The monster's breath is rotten. Her face is to its teeth.

She's so close now, she can feel the percussion in her spine. She inches closer, and her heart in its mouth beats faster. The sound's hypnotic. She's not used to it, but there's something about it. Hard to imagine now, how she existed all those years, oceans away... For a moment, she's back in her office in the Official Residence, toes in the rug, eyes straining. Chest dead silent. Some things are worse than monsters.

This time, she doesn't hesitate. She closes her eyes, and even though her hands won't stop shaking, she lets the intelligence of her body guide her fingers. There's the brush of bone, the tackiness of gums. Her fingers reach deeper. Then she feels it—something vital, electric. She doesn't breathe. It's thumping.

Her fingers can't quite reach around it. She squeezes her wrists through the space between its incisors. Then her elbows. She's in the monster to her armpits. She closes her fingers around her heart. It slows. She exhales.

When the monster's jaw loosens, the Consul isn't expecting the loss of resistance. Her legs slide, and before she can find her footing, she's sprayed in the face by a torrent of water. It knocks her to the ground. She hits her chin on a log and her knee on a rock, but the important thing—she's still holding her heart. Water streams into her boots. The ghost pipe's submerged.

The monster's weeping. It looks smaller without her heart. Now instead of fire in its eyes, there's only loss. Her eyes get wet. She knows what it's like to be in this world without a heart. She has a vision of the beast crying every full moon, drowning the forest in sorrow.

She starts back toward the cabin, but it's slow-going—the monster's tears are to her knees. She has to wade through water, and her soaked boots and pants weigh her down. Her heart thuds in her hand, warm and slimy. She tightens her fingers. She's only gone a few steps when the monster starts moaning. Sorrow cracks the night, and the Consul lets out a sob. She imagines her husband, crying into his brownie batter, and her son, wiping a tear from his book, blurring the print. The monster howls. The whole forest grieves in reply. The sound echoes in her chest and she remembers.

Last time, she stood facing the monster-pup as her child-heart fluttered in its teeth. The pup's eyes were sad. Her eyes filled up too, but she'd made her decision. She felt grown-up. Dragonflies flitted and she swatted them away.

She doesn't want the memory, but now she can't stop it. The monster didn't steal anything. She ripped her heart out by herself. She can still see the blood running between her fingers, the tears filling up her hollowed chest as she turned her back to the forest. She was still blinking, forcing back tears, when the moon came down and drowned them both with its brightness.

Now the water's so high, the Consul has to swim. She's out of shape and out of practice. The heart in her hand makes it harder. Every time the monster howls, the water surges. The world will be submerged by morning. The Consul struggles to keep her chin above water. She reaches out to a tree top and hugs it. Spits out salt water and tries not to go under.

An idea starts to form. There's no time to weigh her options or pull out that chart with the acronyms from the Ministry. Her title and helmet hair can't help her. She has only herself to decide if it's a fair compromise. She'll have to trust her diplomatic instincts, for once be a Consul.

She closes her eyes, and lifts her hand above water. Holding the tree top with her elbow, she opens her other palm wide. The forest goes silent.

The next instant, the monster's bounding to her, each step sloshing the woods. The Consul loses hold of the tree top and goes under in a wave. She swallows salt water and only barely keeps hold of her heart. She's swept left, then right, and upside down. Her lungs burn, there's no air, she can't find the way up. Panic rises, then overwhelming sleepiness. She's about to give in when her head bursts through the surface. By some miracle, she hasn't lost her heart.

She coughs and sputters, starved for air. Her eyes clear, and she's only inches from the monster. It smells of wet dog.

The water's barely to its waist. It extends its arms and its claws reflect moonlight. The Consul's too spent to recoil, and she doesn't have any fear left in her. The monster reaches into her palm and takes her heart with cupped claws. When she looks again, her heart is beating, slow and constant, behind its blood-dripping teeth. The water's already receding.

The monster blinks, and fire returns to its eyes. It tilts its head, its eyes a question. The Consul considers. Can she live with the beast? She brings her hand to her chest. She can't fathom returning to post with that silence. The beast licks its lips and lets out a soft whine. She takes a breath. She's a diplomat, and it is, after all, a compromise.

She nods to the monster, and its arms and its legs bend inward. There's a scraping and a softening of bone, a pop. The monster squeezes its femurs through the narrow space between her ribs, followed by its scapulas and incisors. Once inside the empty space of her chest, it steps in circles to make a bed. The monster curls into a ball, warm and dry, and promptly falls asleep.

Her clothes are dry when she reaches the cabin, though her boots are likely unsalvageable. Her husband's left dinner in the fridge. There's even dessert, a homemade brownie with its own paper plate. He's set a place at the table, with a note that says, "Enjoy." She's surprised at her appetite.

Even though it's past midnight, her husband trades his fuzzy socks for shoes and her son leaves his book in the bedroom. They sit around a campfire, roast marshmallows, and listen for loons in the dark. Her husband sings a camp song and she and her son roll their eyes. They could almost be a family. She goes to bed smelling of salt, smoke, and animal. The moon's full, but she doesn't cry.

The next full moon, the Consul's in her Official Residence office, toes deep in a rug, a pile of documents on her desk. Her cheeks are dry. She's almost through the backlog—she's been catching up in the evenings, after her receptions and dinners.

She signs her name on the paper and writes 'approved'. She sits back in her chair, and something stirs in her chest. She puts her hand to where she used to be hollow and feels the monster inside, breathing. For a moment, she thinks it will leap out of her and show the world those teeth. Instead it sighs, and rolls from its haunches to its side. It gets cramped in there. The monster smacks its lips, then it's back to dreaming forests.

She still doesn't understand how it fits in her. Sometimes she worries that its teeth will slip if she jumps or loses her balance. But she likes when it tells her secrets. Now, when she goes to her dinners, she doesn't care whether her table companions talk to her.

There are complications, but that's to be expected with any compromise. The monster gets stiff when she spends all day at a desk. The Consul's started taking walks at lunch, before her afternoon meetings, so it can stretch. The monster likes birds. So does the Consul. The monster's urges are stronger. She's started to close the blinds in her office to avoid tempting it. The monster has an appetite. She's starting to suspect what it eats. She tries not to think how that sustains her. She tells herself her son was bound to lose his heart anyway, all that time in books. As for her husband... at least now she can bake.

One year later, she's back at the podium, looking down at an audience, at her very own national day. She's in her best helmet, three layers of foundation, and a technicolor blue power suit. She can't remember the last time she wore heels.

There's a hush in the audience. She has the notes her staff prepared, but she's feeling confident, so she keeps them in her pocket and gives her speech off-script. The audience, including the host country Foreign Minister listen, rapt. When she sees a little girl in the audience, she improvises, telling the crowd one day, that little girl will be a Consul. The audience claps, and the little girl beams. A bird, indigo and orange, flies over the stage. The Consul pauses her speech to admire it. No one notices how tightly she grips the podium. The audience waits. She puts a hand to her chest, to quiet the monster, then unrushed, continues to speak.

After the speech, she escapes to the washroom. Stands at the mirror and admires her helmet. She likes the way her foundation's cracked. She parts her lined lips, and her reflection does the same.

Since there's no one else in the washroom, she opens her mouth wider. Looks past her two golden molars and her titanium crown. In the back of her throat, two fire eyes gleam. She tilts her head farther. In the mirror, there's a flash of long teeth, then the percussion of a hundred beating hearts.

The rhythm takes her back to the forest. She breathes in evergreens, and faint fungal rot. The porcelain sink reflects moonlight. Pine trees and saprophytes sprout up in the toilet stalls. Ghost pipe bursts through the sink. The forest thrums with life, electric. The Consul and her beast smile at their reflection. Then, unrushed, they start to recite the secret name of trees.

*See E.C. Dorgan's story "The Beast-Consul"
online at Metaphorosis.
If you liked it, leave a comment. Authors love
that!
Remember to subscribe to our e-mail updates so
you'll know when new stories are posted.*

About the story

I was walking in the woods with my dogs when this story first came to me. I was struck by the image of this character, a woman who cries and cries every full moon without knowing why. My hands were full, and I didn't have a pen or any way to capture it. When I got home, I jotted down what I could remember. I was in the middle of writing another story, and I already had an idea for my next story after that. I thought I could just write a few notes and save this story fragment for another day. The story had other ideas.

The next day when I was out walking, the image came to me again, this time more vivid. Over the following days, I'd be out in the woods and pieces of the story would come to me. The story started to weave together during my walks. I didn't have a pen, but it demanded to be written.

I tried bringing a pen and paper with me a few times, but I was worried about walking into a moose or more likely, a pick-up truck. I gave up, and starting cutting my walks short—rushing home and trying to remember and write down everything. It was early summer, and there were birds and dragonflies everywhere. And the trees were, as always, breathtaking...

Once I got the story down, I was able to walk in the woods in peace again.

A question for the author

Q: What is your favorite word?

A: Lately I've been loving the word 'skyward'. Now when I'm writing, I have to go back through my stories and make sure I'm not over-using it. By some wonder, it's not in "The Beast-Consul."

About the author

E.C. Dorgan writes dreamy dark fantasy and monster stories in Alberta, Canada. She spends too much time wandering in forests and watching birds.

Copyright

Title information

Metaphorosis December 2023

ISSN: 2573-136X (online)
ISBN: 978-1-64076-271-8 (e-book)
ISBN: 978-1-64076-272-5 (paperback)

Copyright

Works of fiction

This book contains works of fiction. Characters, dialogue, places, organizations, incidents, and events portrayed in the works are fictional and are products of the author's imagination or used fictitiously. Any resemblance to actual persons, places, organizations, or events is coincidental.

All rights reserved

Moral rights asserted

Each author whose work is included in this book has asserted their moral rights, including the right to be identified as the author of their respective work(s).

Publisher

Metaphorosis Magazine is an imprint of Metaphorosis Publishing
Neskowin, OR, USA

www.metaphorosis.com

"Metaphorosis" is a registered trademark.

Discounts available

Substantial discounts are available for educational institutions, including writing workshops. Discounts are also available for quantity purchases. For details, contact Metaphorosis at metaphorosis.com/about

Metaphorosis Publishing

Metaphorosis offers beautifully written science fiction and fantasy. Our imprints include:

Metaphorosis Magazine
Plant Based Press
Verdage
Vestige

You can also find us:
Metaphorosis@writing.exchange
@Metaphorosis
www.facebook.com/metaphorosis

Help keep Metaphorosis running by
supporting us at
Patreon.com/metaphorosis

See more about some of our books on the following pages.

Metaphorosis Magazine

Metaphorosis is an online speculative fiction magazine dedicated to quality writing. We publish an original story every week, along with author bios, interviews, and notes on story origins.

We also publish monthly print and e-book issues, as well as yearly Best of and Complete anthologies.

Come and see us online at magazine.Metaphorosis.com.

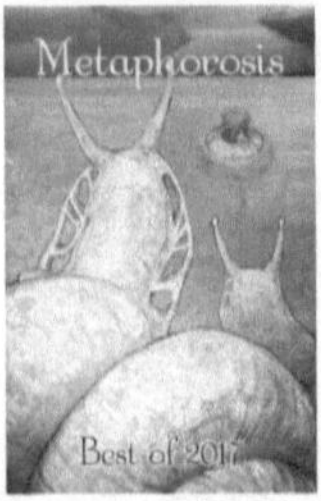

Plant Based Press

plant
based
press

Vegan-friendly science fiction and fantasy, including anthologies of the year's best SFF stories, from 2016-2020.

Chambers of the Heart

*speculative stories
by
B. Morris Allen*

A heart that's a building, a dog that's a program, a woman sinking irretrievably — stories about love, loss, and motion.

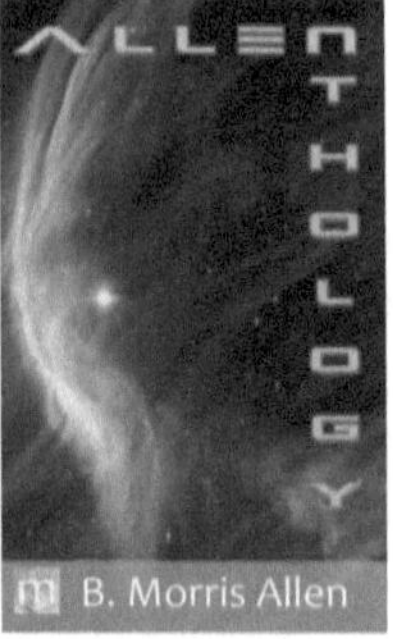

Susurrus

A darkly romantic story of magic, love, and suffering.

Allenthology: Volume I

Including three full collections of SFF stories.

Verdage

Verdage

Science fiction and fantasy books for writers — full of great stories, often with an additional focus on the craft of speculative fiction writing.

Reading 5X5 x3

Changes

How do stories move from 'maybe' to published?

Here are 15 case studies of stories published in *Metaphorosis* magazine.

Reading 5X5 x2

Duets

How do authors' voices change when they collaborate?

A round-robin of five talented science fiction and fantasy authors collaborating with each other and writing solo.

Including stories by Evan Marcroft, David Gallay, J. Tynan Burke, L'Erin Ogle, and Douglas Anstruther.

Score

an SFF symphony

An anthology with an emotional score from the heights of joy to the depths of despair – but always with a little hope shining through.

Reading 5X5

Five stories, five times

See how different writers take on the same material.

Reading 5X5

Writers' Edition

Two extra stories, the story seed, and authors' notes on writing.

Vestige

Novelettes, novellas, and novels by Metaphorosis authors.

The Nocturnals
Mariah Montoya

Night is Dangerous. Day is deadly.

Where day and night last thirty years, humans move constantly stay ahead of the night and cruel Nocturnals that call it home. But a boy is lost out there.

Joyful Heave

Science fiction and fantasy anthologies with innovative and unusual themes.

Museum Piece
an unusual collection

A gallery of the strange and outrageous

Step right up and enter a world of wonder and oddities! These museums are not your typical tourist traps. From the Museum of Lost Dreams to the Suicide Museum, each exhibit will take you on a journey you won't soon forget.

www.ingramcontent.com/pod-product-compliance
Lightning Source LLC
Chambersburg PA
CBHW030427120726
47903CB00003B/839